Another Book About Another Broken Heart

Julia Tausch

Another Book About Another Broken Heart
© 2003 Julia Tausch
Edited and designed by Andy Brown

Muffin photo by Maggie Maloney and Jesse Foster
Other photos by Andy Brown
First Edition

National Library of Canada Cataloguing in Publication

Tausch, Julia, 1978-
        Another book about another broken heart / Julia Tausch.

ISBN 1-894994-00-0

        I. Title.

PS8589.A8742A76 2003   C813'.6   C2003-905172-2

conundrum press
PO Box 55003 CSP Fairmount
Montreal, Quebec
H2T 3E2, Canada
conpress@ican.net
http://home.ican.net/~conpress

Printed in Quebec on recycled paper.

This book was produced with the financial assistance of the
Canada Council for the Arts and the Department of Canadian
Heritage through IPOLC.

**Canada Council
for the Arts**

**Conseil des Arts
du Canada**

I deserve some credit. Or at least an edit.
Take out the part that breaks my heart.

—Sloan

To my parents for the love, the support, and the laughs.

I swore that I would never write another word about another broken heart. Then I left the love of my life and moved to a brand new city to start again, cold, fresh, drained, rinsed clean—words used to describe canned tuna. In my intro to acting class in my first year of university, my hugely jaded, wannabe intimidating, leggings-clad instructor archly told us in his fake British accent, "There are only three motivations in life that count: flight, fight, or fuck." This made no sense to me until last week. I flew. I couldn't have done it without the buzz of an overnight train and my parents' frenetic assurance that this is all for the best and now I'm spending my days walking to and from Canadian Tire. I'm buying shelving units, papertowel racks, shower curtain hooks, a hammer, some nails, a set of screwdrivers, a yellow rug, a broom and a dustpan, a frying pan, a toaster oven, taking back the toaster oven because it doesn't broil (but when do I broil?), spatula, a set of knives, shoe-rack, doormat, sheets, a microwave (lucky thing my neighbour helped me carry it upstairs, unlucky that he's cute because I will never write another word about another broken heart).

I've put on eyeshadow and have sat down to write. It's nice to wear a bit of makeup while writing I think. Get into character, release Yourself, whatever that is, let Yourself keep going, keep dwelling on the fact that You up and left Brian, let Yourself plan the menu for the week, think of new ways of serving black beans. The new shell, with its shimmery eyeshadow and its frosted lips will show the body how to pound a better life into Microsoft Word and before You know what's happened, when You're still all blustery and annoyed and pulling at the cold cream nesting in your unsuccessfully de-mascara-ed lashes, that better life, shiny like Your fake face was, will sit there in the computer smiling, just waiting to be noticed the next day and celebrated with a fresh batch of line notes and half a nervous breakdown concerning narrative structure.

I believe I have written myself into a feminized space a hysterical space. Should go well with the yellow rug.

My apartment building (found within one sore-footed day of my arrival) is attached to the building next to it by a network of fire escapes. In the space on the ground an ugly oblong of dirt and sharp gravel is populated by thin, patchy squirrels trying to scrape together a living from the tenants' garbage collecting on the fire escape landings. My landlord calls this space "the courtyard."

An old man lives across this trashyard from me and he swears most mornings in long heated bouts at the world, he screams, "What the fuck is going on?" And I sit bolt upright in bed and listen and a small half-moon shaped part of my brain hopes that soon he'll be evicted. I can't believe I think it but I hope he'll be evicted. I don't want him to have his own apartment to walk around in his briefs, or lie shirtless on the floor watching his broken TV set that delivers fuzzy shows in a sick green colour. I want him to stand, sit and sleep on a street corner like the other elderly mentally ill who have been evicted, so that he will swear in long heated bouts at passers-by. But of course that's just a miniscule part of my brain. The rest of it is just scared as hell to be living alone and asks the same question as he does: "What the fuck is going on?"

The love thing was pretty beautiful. Love made us entitled to spend money and be lavish. Bourgeois behaviour without the guilt. We'd buy brie cheese and wine. I liked the brie rinds and Brian didn't, so he'd hollow out the creamy middles of the cheese chunks with a knife or a finger and give me the white, crusty shell. Cast off cheese cocoons. We'd sit on the living room carpet and eat.

We had a living room and a bedroom and a small extra room with a hanging plant and we were within walking distance of the College subway station. The apartment was near the bar where Brian worked but it was a pain in the ass for me to get to Kinko's, my place of employment. Compromise, this was called. I had learned from my father that compromise was the key to a successful and enduring love life. From my mother I had learned to fight, tooth and nail.

We paid a thousand.

"Each?" people would ask, voices squeaking at the edge. Eating a devilled egg at the parties we threw.

"Together."

"That's not so bad," people would say.

Last night I went to an Indian restaurant three minutes from my house. I wanted to treat myself. Doing it alone felt subversive and sexy. Lavish and bourgeois without the guilt, but without the love crutch. So basically just bourgeois, but last night it felt subversive and I wore lipstick, threw a wink at the post-feminism in my mirror and strutted down the street carrying a *Cosmo* (my dinner guest).

The Indian waiter with a slight but confused British accent told the table next to my cute table-for-one that he's not much for curries. He prefers fish and chips or a steak. The diners laughed and looked at each other with old, knowing, watery blue eyes. Their wrinkles smiled with them. When the waiter was gone they said to each other: "That was cute."

"Yes, that was good."

I wondered why the waiter lied. Not much for curries. Nice try, buddy.

Today I finagle an interview at the Second Cup. I just walk right in and smile big and ask them (in French) if they need me. Not if they need help, but if they need me. It's sort of exciting. Again, wearing lipstick. I'm a drag queen in Montreal. I'm sure I'm passing. The manager smiles at me, a warm kind of smile. She's forty-five or so, maybe older. Her hair is gray and tied into a neat little knot at the bottom of her Second Cup baseball cap. I'm sure she's thinking I'm the kind of cosmopolitan youth she'd die to employ. My hair (bleached, with two inch roots) puffs electric around my head, a buzzing, tarnished halo, an ailing neon sign. The manager looks at me, smile fading and asks in English five times better than my French, "Will you work until two AM?"

"Yeah!" That's right. I say it with an exclamation mark. I feel the lipstick slide off my face, smack the tiled floor. Though I'm suddenly nakedly Ontarian, she gives me an interview. Two-thirty tomorrow. AM or PM? I ask her. Her laugh is disarmingly tinkling, like a four-year old beauty queen's.

"Afternoon! I'm never here for the night shift!" This time, she's the one who uses the exclamation mark.

The grocery store is just three minutes down the road from my new place. Across from the Indian restaurant. This is mind-bogglingly convenient, and I go to stock up. I buy canned goods to put into my Canadian Tire plastic shelving unit. Filling it pleases me greatly. The drawers on the unit are transparent and I can see my canned corn and tuna and pineapple and lentils and bags of noodles and juice-boxes and three kinds of tea looking out at me. They are watching over me, the contents of my humble larder.

Brian would despise my new hoarding habit. He always made fun of his grandmother for keeping stacks of useless-ness in cans in her basement.

"Who needs that many pickled beets? And cream of cel-ery soup. No one even *likes* cream of celery!"

"She lived through the war!" I always said. I like Brian's grandmother. She asked me once, with her wrinkled, spot-ted hand on my knee, if I enjoyed oral sex.

"Giving or receiving?" I asked.

Brian's grandmother laughed and laughed, like I'd told her a great joke. Her eyes teared up, her leathery skin moved over the muscles working in her face. Brian came in with our Pepsis, just as his grandmother said, "We didn't think much about receiving in my day."

"You couldn't dream?"

She started laughing afresh, tears rolling down her cheeks.

Will I ever see Brian's grandmother again?

I get the job at the Second Cup. Isabelle, the lady with the knot of gray hair, makes me speak in French in my interview

11

and I feel famous, like I'm on French TV after winning my Olympic sport and the viewers at home find me cute and feel nationally flattered that I'm giving French such a good go. I stumble, largely in the *passé composé*, around the ideas that I'm hard-working and committed and really like the non-smoking atmosphere.

Isabelle asks whether I'll be starting at Concordia or at McGill come September and I tell her that I'm starting at neither. I've decided to take a year off school since ditching my half-completed program at York in favour of fleeing the city overnight.

"No school at all?" Isabelle asks, raising her well-plucked brows. She is apparently distrustful of those willing to work in her establishment without larger goals.

I try to rally and overzealously promise to work as hard as a stuntwoman. It's the fanciest French word I can remember from highschool: *la cascadrice*. I shouldn't have said it, it made no sense grammatically or rhetorically. Isabelle gives me an overt scowl and says that in Quebec, the term is *le stuntman*. That's all there is. She nevertheless hands me the job, an apron and a ballcap and tells me I can start training now.

I pull my ball cap over my puff of hair, the milk-steaming machine sputters and pops. "Just *le stuntman*," I say. "Isn't that interesting?"

"Yes." Isabelle's smile has tightened into something impersonal and polite. I have been hired, hailed, a brand new worker subjectivity to add to my list, right under ex-lover.

I feel depressed. My fridge smells like farts. I eat sliced dill-pickles right out of the jar with my fingers trying to satisfy my craving for General Tao's chicken that I can't afford. It just so happens that the city's second best General Tao's chicken (so voted by the most fascist of the Montreal news-papers) is made mere blocks from my apartment. I have begun to believe that my bachelor apartment with its slop-ing floors and its cracked stucco walls is in fact the official centre of the universe. But since I spent the majority of my summer earnings on furnishings, canned goods and Indian food I will have to wait for Isabelle's first cheque before I sample the chicken.

It's time to admit that I haven't been outside a ten block radius of my home. I want to scream at someone that I thought it would be different. I thought moving to a new city would be new, that I could just slice it open like a grape-fruit, all those moist, sweet sections beckoning me to grab a toothy spoon and dig right in, scoop up the meat of this town, feel the membranes burst and pop between my teeth, let the juice run out. I was so prepared for anything, any-thing but my fart-smelling fridge and my vinegary fingers at two AM on a Friday.

Every second or third day, I phone my mom and dad to see how our beloved guinea pig is doing and to whine. My par-ents were extreme advocates of my move to Montreal to rid myself of the shackles of monogamy, which is how my mom, on more than one occasion, supposedly in jest, referred to my relationship with Brian. I think it's always been a bit of a sore spot for her that she fell so hard for my father when she did. She didn't really want to do a whole lot besides hang out with him and be in love and he didn't really want much else either, which prevented my mom from living the life I suspect she'd always wanted. I admit, this assumption is not based on much, but at least once a year she tells me about these silver stiletto boots she saw in a store window in early 1980. By that time she was already two months pregnant with me and, the way she tells the story, she acknowledged the impracticality of the boots and beamed with pride. Then she says something like, "But in retrospect…" and that's when the story invariably trails off. Sometimes she pulls out her Sister Sledge record on nights like those and bops around the living room in that heartbreakingly earnest way that only mothers can bop.

The goddamn gull-squack, every morning squacking at me *you live in south eastern Canada with summers that drench you in sweat and glue you to your sheets.* Fucking gull-squack, in the mornings hailing another day of heat and damp and blazing sunshine bouncing off office towers and stinky armpits and sunburnt eyes. Gull-squack gull-squack it's time it was confessed, Brian wrote a poem once that had these words in it, "the gull-squack," and I took note and kept the note handy, in case I ever should need it. I guess I need it now, I guess I feel some kind of a need to be close to Brian. Good God, who am I kidding? I miss him like crazy. And why hasn't he called? Why hasn't he called my parents to get my number, demanded that I come back baby come back home come back baby the hanging plant is dying. The fact that Brian calls me baby on a regular basis

should be embarrassing but I find it endearing. The fact
that he hasn't called could denote respect for my decision
to leave him but I feel fucking shafted. I have begun obsessing. That may be the reason why every detail of my new
stupid life including the fart smelling fridge has been men-
tioned so far except for the fact that I love Brian. Jesus
Christ, do I love Brian. Brian I take you, even the thought
of you with the reckless abandon and the paranoid guilt
and the worshiping, toe-curling relish of an addict. I know
that I'm wobbling dangerously close to the edge of a
Robert Palmer reference here, but you know what? Might
as *well* face it. And he sits in my mirror, too. I look at
myself and I see myself with him. I wear outfits that he'd
like and I smile in this way that I do that he thinks is cute
where I bite my lower lip, and I do it in the mirror because
he's *there* somehow. And I'm looking, I'm looking for a
new way to live, trust me, that's why I came here in the
first place, to get out of this obsession this desperation this
need for him and I look at other boys, I do! But they're all
methadone and I'm not a fool I know what I want I
thought that's what we girls are supposed to know god-
dammit I know what I want and it's you so can you just.
Fucking. Give. Me. One. More.

I live just off of Ste. Catherine Street in beautiful, downtown Montreal, just minutes from grocery shopping, banks, restaurants, boutiques, nightclubs, jazz clubs, pubs, bars, two universities and so much more. The street seems to run forever and it runs, it burns with adrenaline and hype and need. It is exciting to live in this town, it is begging for me, it is begging for my art, it is begging me to walk, nay strut its streets. It yearns for me to turn its corners and frequent its shops. I am walking home from work with a Walkman on my head grooving to electro-feminist post-punk and I feel that I may be, at this moment, the walking sign of our goddamn times. I've had a coffee. I don't drink it much. I've hit nirvana for sure I've reached heaven found elysium discovered the meaning of it all and then I crash. Gray, gum-stained sidewalks flank the wide street clotted with maniacs honking and squealing round bends. The countless non-denominationally Asian restaurants perfume the air with rancid oil and bok choy refuse rotting out back. It is July first and the sky is the colour of fresh paper smudged by a kid's inky hand.

Tonight I am the farty one and not my fridge. I can remember nights this farty spent with Brian when I had to implode them all. I never farted in front of him, not after a whole year. That's not entirely true. There was this night we went to this wedding. It was my kindergarten best friend's wedding. I had the most vile gas ever experienced. Seriously. And I let it out periodically the whole day that we spent together. I know he knows. But I've never said a thing about it. Even on our drive home I farted in the car, Brian called me on it and I deflected. I anecdoted about mystery farters instead.

"You know that little vestibule in the place where I used to live with Kara?"

"Yeah."

"Sometimes we'd come home or be going out and it would reek in there. We had a mystery farter!" (This much was true.) "He must have come into your car." (This much was not.)

"Our stove in the old house used to fart. Swear to God." And so on and so forth. Who buys this crap? I'll tell you who buys it. The flimsy-thin fabric of love is made from this kind of shit.

"Hi Brian, it's just me calling. Um. I guess my number's on the Call ID so. Call me. When you get a chance. Bye."

I broke down I did it I called him I broke down. I left a message. Moron! Now I can sit in my apartment for the rest of my life trying to distract myself with my meager supply of stuff waiting waiting waiting. My food, my CDs. I've taken four showers, I'm not joking. I'm shrivelled! When the water hits the drain cover in a certain way it sounds a tiny little bit like a phone and I go crazy, my eyes rip open, my nostrils flare, my head bobs up up up like a dog, sniffing out that sound. That sound. It doesn't come. Not today. Not today. But it could. It's four AM. I haven't left the house for nine hours. It took moving myself a province away to discover that love is a panopticon. Discipline and punish. There's something about those words that makes me smack my lips and hope for more.

"I'm sorry. I didn't know you knew."

Next morning. He has called back. This is what he's said. I want to barf.

"Knew what?" I don't want to know what. I have the cold-wet-balled-up-chunk-of-old-dirty-rags kind of dread in my stomach. "Knew what? Brian?"

"That I cheated on you. I was cheating on you. You knew. That's why you left."

"What?" This has a hard shell but it's runny in the middle.

"You moved out. You were gone. I feel like shit but you did the right thing. I deserved it."

"I. I didn't know, Brian."

"What?"

"I." And then the tears come. And then the sobbing. And then the snot. "I didn't know." I look around my room, and at my sweaters neatly folded, stacked one on top of the other on a shelf. A green one a pink one a purple one a yellow one another green one. I hate them, I hate wool, for Christ's sake what is the POINT? I picture myself naked on a beach, flaying off my own skin with oyster shells, where did I learn to picture something like this, snot drips onto my receiver. Plastic? What the fuck? Who invents this shit and why?

"I. I'm so sorry, Katy." We both just breathe for a few seconds, me more wetly than him. "Oh fucking shit. Why did you leave then? You left overnight. I figured you must have found out. I mean. Why did you go?"

"I don't know," I sob. "I have no idea. I was just. I was just so afraid."

"Of what?"

My answer hits me surprisingly fast. "That you didn't

love me the same as I love you." I'm talking really quietly. I wish I could yell or shriek or something. What's the protocol for cuckolds nowadays?

"Oh," he says.

"Is that all you can say?" I feel a little anger kicking in.

"I don't know what to say. I. Christ. I'm so sorry. I didn't mean. Oh God, I don't want to hurt you."

"How many times?" I say. "Was it just once? I can forgive just once."

"It wasn't just once. I'm sorry. It. It's been going on for a little longer than a month. We always used condoms though, you don't have to worry."

How sweet. "The same girl?"

"The same girl. She's—"

"Don't tell me who she *is*, Brian. Christ!" My stomach feels like I've consumed four raw chickens in the last half hour. "I just. I don't understand how. How did I not know? How. How could you?"

"Oh God, Katy. I don't know. I felt so bad the whole time. I'm such an asshole. I. I don't know what else to say."

"Are you. You know. *With* her now?" I shouldn't have asked, I know I don't want to know the answer. I shut my eyes and clench my fists.

"Yeah. I am."

"Oh my God."

"I'm sorry."

"I have to go, Brian. I think I'm gonna throw up."

"Katy—"

Beep. I've actually hung up. I don't think I've ever hung up on anyone before in earnest. All I want to do now is call him right back, straight away, hear his voice again, beg him to tell me what I did wrong. But I really think that I might be sick so I just sit on my bed and rock back and forth and make a little simpering noise. I try to breathe.

The thing I was trying to run from had already happened. Long ago. More than a month. I don't understand. I was running away from a potentiality for Christ's sake, scared away by a tiny, slippery, vague notion that maybe, just maybe Brian wouldn't think I was perfect forever. That barely audible whisper was enough to drive me from my home. Turns out it had already become real-life, quick and kinetic. He'd already stopped loving me. To love somebody else! And the whole time that hanging plant hung there knowing and watching me commit the gross disgusting despicable sin of card-making. It's true! I sat there, under the plant, at the little desk with its peeling cherry veneer, the window open, kids from low-income families playing road hockey outside in sweatpants. Four weeks ago. I made him a card. I sat there listening to the kids screaming "car" and I drew a little egg man with my markers and wrote his name on top in bubble letters and wrote things about love, and even about kissing on the inside in pen. Just because. He was my little egg man. He could make anything with eggs—poached, scrambled, fried, devilled (for our parties), Benedict—you name it. My little egg man. The embarrassment! The burning hell of shame that comes with this memory, it makes my hands fly up, my fingers press to my eyes, aching to gouge them out, to do anything anciently symbolic of penance for my own cowish stupidity. I fling myself onto the bed. This will have to do for now. I need my eyes. I have less than an hour before I have to be at work.

I want to get drunk tonight. Man, I've gotta get pissed. I mean I want to get hosed soused weave like a mad, animate meat cleaver hard and sharp through the night. I try all day to make people from work come out. I've just met them! But I ask them. Try to be casual, try to play the new girl card, just trying to make friends.

"Anybody wanna go for a beer tonight?" *Wanna.* That's casual. "I thought I might check out Brutopia. I hear they have cheap beer." I'm just up for a deal. You know how it is. It's not like I desperately need out of my head for just a couple of hours, just a minute really for God's sake do none of you latté steaming GEEKS even drink? Good fuck! But thank God all that text is realized only as a twitchy eye. A twitchy eye the only hint pointing to my utter loss of sanity, my insta-alcoholism. Today all day when Celine Dion comes on the radio I have to go to the bathroom and let some tears out. Fuck you Brian, you *were* my strength when I was weak. Twitch twitch. How about those oyster shells? Anyway.

I get drunk. Man, I get pissed. I get hosed. I try to keep it together. At Brutopia. With Janet from my work, the only one who comes along.

Janet: warm, friendly, super sincere. You wouldn't believe how nice this girl is to all the customers. Even when they're like "but I didn't *ask* for whipped cream" which is when I say "yes you did" and hand them the drink anyway. The weird thing is they usually take it. Janet's not like that. She's all "No problem" and "You bet!" *You bet!* She's cute, with a round little face and a chin that juts out and when I ask if she'd like to go for a beer later she says, "Fuck yes."

We talk about our smiles, work versus real life, the real life one creeping back into our musculature as the beer worms warmly through our organs through our blood.

"The real life one has an edge, a curl, a borderline sneer that acknowledges the fact that life actually sucks. When I'm at work it's a game I play, like I'm a robot from the future programmed not to know the big secret. I just go about the work like it's tacit knowledge that shit is wonderful, that people should be happy to pay four dollars for a shot of espresso with some whipped cream and carcinogens mixed in. If I'm a robot, I can do it." This is Janet talking. She had seemed so genuinely abubble earlier at work. I mention this and she smiles. Definitely a real life one.

We talk about how she's been going to Concordia for the past three years for film and history and that she's lived in Montreal all her life. I tell her that I did English for two years at York, but I moved here after I dumped my boyfriend.

"I'm happy with an assortment of flings and random fucks," she says. "Boyfriends are too much of a pain in the ass."

"Yeah, I know what you mean," I say. "I just found out that mine has been cheating on me since, like, forever!" Here we go, four beers and as many hours later, Janet has become an intimate knower of my life, my Brian, my little egg man, my life.

"Wow," she says when I get to the part about how I was a bit of a late bloomer and lost my virginity to him last year. "Oh boy." Which is pretty much what I thought at the time.

When I was a little girl I was deathly afraid that I would become addicted to cocaine.

Let me show you something. This is me sitting on my bed with Brian. We met maybe a week ago. This! This here is the huge wodge of nerves and excitement flexing and unflexing and being generally wobbly and disgusting in the middle of me. See how it shimmers in the light? There's Brian getting up. He's smiling at me. He's changing the CD. I'm talking, I won't shut up.

"Did I tell you about my friend Sabrina's Aqua Velva phase? She used to wear it like perfume. She kept a little bottle in her purse. She'd put it on, then wink. She actually winked constantly at the time. Wink wink wink…" I'm unconsciously obsessively firing words out into the air which has become strange and electric and zingy. There's Brian walking over to change the CD, there's Brian walking over and sitting on me. I'm sitting on the edge of my bed with the frantic, growing word bubble sitting phosphorescent and dangerous over my head and Brian sits on me like a lap dancer, his skinny knees digging into me, his weight on me the best feeling I've felt since birth. The whole thing is tinged with sleaziness and gender mischief and and and he's kissing me. Mmm! The words are gone and I can feel his tongue and he can feel mine (according to logic, what's logic?) and he's touching my sweatered breasts and now we're lying down and I look up at him mad goofily and he looks down at me the same. The same! Never ever before has this… oh but wait, oh he catches my lip in his teeth and bites and sucks and it makes a sound and we laugh and he asks me how the hell you undo this bra anyway and I, who has never known a man's hands, who has never before known the heaven, the pure unadulterated connection with the celestial that one's lip caught in another's teeth will cause, whip my sweater off whip my bra off and suddenly half-naked I become aware that I am a generator of lust that I hold this capability that these breasts that had stood so proud and perky and fine, just fine! on their own for so many years pull triggers in another person's head and hands and heart. And he touches them, snuggles his face against them, kisses them and I lie there, in my bed in my room with Bob Dylan on and the bright posters on the walls. I try to listen to the music, I make a few happy little noises. He undoes my button-fly jeans and he kisses my belly and I laugh—how could this not cause hysteria each and every time?—pop pop pop go the buttons. Is he trying to unbutton them slowly? To be sexy? Is he—haah-thinking about this? Because I'm not ha ha ha I'm just living the moment. Kissing my hips—what the hell should I do with the rest of my body when he's all the way down there—kissing my underpants because he pulled the jeans down and suddenly I have an itch, a burn and compulsion to pull those pants all the way off because otherwise I'm just a spent piece of used jet trash, lying there with my pants around my knees, whore complex whore complex! Why the fuck can't I shut this thing off?

Look at what's happening here! Every little patch of my skin being kissed is becoming beautiful. That's how it works. Brian's lips say hey little patch of skin I appreciate you and then the patch shines and beams radiantly ready for more compliments which he even doles out! "You're so soft," Brian says and kisses my lips as if they might be responsible for the production of the rest of my body, my silky smoothie sexy body please do MORE!

So here's where words can't do it, it invariably devolves into badness. I know it does because everyone who's anyone has tried before. Breasts have worked, sensual embraces, sure, but start talking point blank, unapologetically about genitalia and you lose. It's too much. You spin into a Victorian-era frenzy, you look away from the page, maybe at your own chaste shoulder, you look back because you want it. But you know you don't want it like this—Brian starts to kiss my vagina. Gross. Brian licks my snatch. Uh huh. Brian gently probes my glistening scarlet and carmine folds with his flexed, hungry tongue, pausing indefinitely at the throbbing pink corpuscle that forms the apex of my soft and ready delta. Okay. This is seriously embarrassing. Isn't it? I mean, even to write it. But you know how it feels. Probably. And I was afraid I'd become addicted to cocaine.

God, I wish I'd never called. Before I called him I had something to live for and that something was the thought that I would just live here in Montreal and be cool and independent and rad and then when I was good and convinced that I could easily live on my own, that I didn't *need* him (or when I couldn't possibly take another minute without him warm and cuddly beside me), I would call him up and tell him that I was sorry but that this was just something that had to be done and now I would move on back to Toronto and we would live near College station in eternal and everlasting love.

Now what? What the fuck now? I sit in the twenty-four hour McDonald's eating a simulacrum of a hot fudge sundae. The many McDonald's in Montreal are different from the McDonald's in sporty, lacquered Ontario. They're dingy here, you can smell the greasy rot coming from the garbage cans, you can feel an oily french fry film on the swiveling chairs, there are tacky ketchup patches on the barely wiped tabletops (tacky like slightly sticky, not like kitch or camp). It's all very European-gone-American-but-still-in-Canada-so-different-again. Longstoryshort it's dirty and disgusting and I feed myself the melting mess of carageenan and reheated choco-shellac and really truly believe, in this moment, that this is the closest I will ever come to sex again in my vacuous, sorry life.

And then I see an old man sitting there by himself eating a combo. A combo! The fries, the drink, the burger, a full meal! Oh the pathos of the combo. This isn't just a snack, like "man, I could use some fries," this is like "well, might as well go someplace for dinner." This is his dinner and he is sitting there, eating it. Picking up fries, dipping them into the small paper cup of ketchup. Intermittently taking a bite of his burger, chewing. He's wearing a long-sleeved golf shirt, tucked into his jeans. He has a belt on. I imagine him sitting at home, probably an apartment of a modest size, clean but not stylish, threading his belt through the beltloops of those jeans. Maybe he has a record playing in the background, or worse, the jazz program on CBC2. That he has to think about these things, all by himself, to tuck in his shirt, to do up his belt, to do his laundry, to eat a meal, these simple things he has to do alone where Normal People do them together, these things destroy me. It's as if he's performing a parody of the fundamentals of living, brutally exposing the silliness and futility of basic existence when another person isn't present to validate these banal functions: "Yeah, I like the pepper bacon burger, I wish they would make this a permanent item." "I think that you look cute in your green shorts, the ones with the bulky pockets, you look like a toddler but in a good way." "Have you read this book? It will rock your forehead." Without these utterances that justify, that indeed *constitute* the mundane, does living not become a mere shadow of what is socially referred to and conceived of as Life? The man opens up the Big Mac, puts on extra ketchup, puts the top bun back on and pushes down a little bit and I wipe my eyes on the rough napkin printed with that mocking bastard clown, smudging his smile with a punishing streak of tear-emulsified mascara.

"Rough night?" accuses Janet. Six AM. Opening shift.

Rough.

I stumbled out of bed at five thirty-seven, threw open the shower curtain, cranked the hot water, cried, allowed my nose to run freely and—yes! It's true!—*vomited* in the shower, a biley, yellow stream of compacted hot fudge and soft-served moot desire whirling down the drain, inspiring self-loathing and masses of self-pity oh! and then there's self-loathing again, the Self! What an asshole.

I pulled on my black pants and my golf shirt and rammed the tails into the waist band and bloused the shirt out again, just like Isabelle instructed me to do during my training. Pushed through the door, into the July dawn, the rising sun a seething, burning eye, rife with disease. There are mornings when I like nothing better than to be among the first awake and walking through the pre-buzz town. This morning is different. I took a creative writing workshop once where we had to read some really conservative but really appealing, really comforting narrative theory that said that a short story's beginning is its most important part. *It should establish the habitual of the world of the story. Following this establishment comes the "then" moment. "Every day Janie went to the end of her street at ten AM and waited for the mail to be delivered. THEN one Thursday she decided not to go."* Ooh! Why? What changed? What led up to this quintessential moment?

And here it is. In evidence. Sweet sweet naturalized narrative structure imposing itself on my life—what I thought was sharp and original reality, so fresh and different from Canadian short fiction for Christ's sake! But no. The "then moment" of Brian Johnson's cheat has converted me from smart, together, moderately obsessive twenty-first-century twenty-something *chick* to something small and sour who pukes in the shower, who bitterly describes the world around her as "rife with disease." The sun has conjunctivitis. How tragic.

"You could say rough morning," I say. "I barfed."

That night Janet and I decide to have a good old fashioned wallow because she has declared that I look like shit. I do not disagree. I barfed again at work. I found myself cutting my eyes at all the girl customers because they might look like the girl Brian's—. Stop. I can't even put it into words. Not yet. The wound is—it's wallow time. So we go. We decide to do it at her house so that I can have a change of scenery and I have really no idea what is going on, I just nod and feel the bend and tease of pity and fledgling friendship.

"We are going to the depanneur and we are getting you some fucking chocolate." Says Janet.

"Uh huh."

We go to the dep below her building and the white light and whirring noise of the finger printed glass-doored fridges momentarily calm my love-fried coffee-varnished nerves.

"Popcorn?"

"Okay."

"Fritos?"

"Yes please."

"Two Fruit and Nuts."

"Yeah. I like Fruit and Nuts. And how about Coke? And Wink."

"Jesus. We're gonna get fat, eh?"

"Yeah. We're gonna waddle into work tomorrow morning." It is here that I cleverly begin to affect a hickish Southern accent and indicate excess girth with my arms.

"Mornin Isabelle, we was just havin us a slumba pahty."

Then two things happen at the same time.

1. Two girls walk in, both slightly bigger than Janet and I, a weight that would prevent them from becoming super models, indeed models of any kind, but would not relegate them to that shame of womandom, that dizzying vortex known as the Plus Size.

2. I say—and it's one of those moments where everything slows down, everything gets blurry and starts to vibrate—I say (OUT LOUD) I say, "Cause being fat means you're stupid." And Janet laughs.

29

The girls look at us, raise their eyebrows, look at each other and repeat it. Word for word.

"Cause being fat means you're stupid."

See, see, see but wait! The reason that Janet is laughing is because she sees the wit here, she knows that I am being sardonic and critical and generally brilliant, I am creating *satire* right here in Marc's Depanneur and I am not I AM NOT poking fun at poundage, we are not two skinny girls skewering the rotund in the broad light of day.... Dammit, these words dig a hole all around me.

We shuffle out of there with lopsided smiles and a plastic bag full of sugar, fat and salt.

"Do you think they think I meant it?" Do ya?

"Absolutely." Says Janet. She has this way of saying things that's like a case of beer thunking down on a counter.

I look at Janet. She's short. She has thick little legs and small hands and shapely, tanned arms. She has big breasts. Did I offend her, too? Did I cut my only tie?

"But that was fuckin funny and so not your fault," she says. "They probably think we're two skinny bitches slumming for the night. Two bulimics ready for a big barf party!" I see her face shudder with recollection of my recent run-ins with vomit. "Sorry," she says.

We take the elevator up to her place in sheepish silence and for about a minute and a half I forget about Brian and feel a spastic, desperate, flailing connection to my half of the humans.

"Hi, Brian?"

This is the night after I, engorged with chocolate, swore

and proclaimed to Janet that I would never ever speak to "that fuck" Brian Johnson ever again.

"Hi. How are you?"

"Miserable."

Silence. How can he be silent? I begin to cry. Snarfle.

"I'm sorry."

"You're sorry."

"Look. I have to go. I don't think this is good for you."

"Don't you fucking EVER tell me what's good for me! You fuck." I am doing what may be referred to as shrieking by a particularly harsh and unfeeling narrator.

It degenerates further. It isn't pretty. Suffice it to say I become a leaky parody of a human and I just can't seem to stop myself. I'll take you to the beginning of the end.

"Who *is* she?" The "is" is far more shrill than italics could ever imply.

"Do you really want to know?"

"Of course! Of course." Pathetic wheezing here.

"Do you remember Amber from my work?"

"Yes."

"Her."

And here I should let him go, I should hang up and be a good girl but instead the following:

"Why her and not me? Why her and not me? Why her and not me? Why her and not me? Why her and not me? Why her and not me? Why her and not me? Why her and not me? Why her and not me? Why her and not me? Why her and not me? Why her and not me? Why her and not me? Why her and not me? Why her and not me? Why her and not me? Why her and not me? Why her and not me? Why her and not me? Why her

31

and not me? Why her and not me? Why her? Why her? Why her? Why her? Why her? Why her? Why her? Why her? Why her?" (I'm paraphrasing.)

And after all of that, he's still there. Isn't he sweet? He didn't even hang up! So I ask him if I'd been better at the sex part, if things would have been different.

People tell me I'm good at writing about The Material. I have an ear for linguistic rhythms. I have an eye for detail. They say. That styrofoam cup with the babyteeth marks sitting on top of the garbage can in front of the Metro station? Got it! The super-squishy high luxury paper towels they have at the golf club where your cousin got married? In the bag! But what about love? How does one exorcise the ephemeral? Does stacking words up in chunky hard bricks of materialism allow defined emotions to seep out from the cracks like so much gloopy mortar? Does obsessing over what's Not It get us any closer to what It is? Does describing the snot coming out of my nose bring the snot-triggering anguish any closer to home? Where is home?

"So last night I was hanging out with my friend Lee? You know the guy. He comes in sometimes. He's really hot? Glasses?" Janet is kind of whispering and her eyebrows are doing a little conspiratorial dance. We are on our ten-thirty break.

"Yeah, I think I know. The guy with the little cap sometimes?"

"Yeah! Him. So anyway. We've been friends for years, me and Lee. He's wicked. He's funny and he's really nice and, I don't know. We just have this really big connection. Like, sometimes we won't see each other for years and then we do again and all of the sudden we're hanging out like all the time. So anyway, last night we're hanging—oh yeah, and also he has a girlfriend who's on exchange in Stockholm right now, some summer design course or something, she's coming back in December. So you need to know that— right. So last night we're hanging out and just watching TV and stuff and it's fun, you know, and he's a really cuddly guy so he has his head like on my legs and I'm playing with his hair and stuff but that's nothing, it's totally normal. So we're just talking and whatever and then we realize that Lee totally missed the last Metro, right? So I was like 'Oh, do you want to sleep over?' because he has before and stuff, so he says sure. So we hang out some more and—we're not drinking or anything either, just so you know. And he's telling me how hot he's always thought I was, you know? Like really genuinely. And he's being realistic about it too you know, like acknowledging the fact that not every guy is into stumpy little short girls with big boobs and thighs."

"I think you're super beautiful," I say, genuinely shocked that there was any question in Janet's mind.

"Yeah, thanks. But you know, no offence, it's a lot more exciting when a really hot man tells me."

"Oh, I know." I know.

"So he's telling me I'm so hot and I'm like 'thanks' and probably blushing and stuff, but still. This is normal. He's always like this. He could charm the pants off... off... I don't know, a Mormon. Right. So then we go to bed and we're just lying there and I'm thinking that I'm really glad that we're hanging out lately and then I feel his hand on my breast!"

"What?"

"Yeah. And at first I thought maybe he wasn't doing it on purpose, like maybe he was already asleep or whatever. But then no. He's definitely, unquestionably touching me. So I turn around and kind of stare at him and he stares back and kind of gives this 'sorry' smile. So then we're just lying there again and I can't believe it but whatever. I mean, it's not like I'd be opposed to sleeping with him or anything, but he has a girlfriend and I won't do that. And he knows that, too, we've totally talked about that kind of stuff. But then he does it again! And I think he's joking right, because who does that? Like. We already stopped it. But then he's back. And this time it doesn't stop so quickly either. And he's sort of like moving behind me. You know, like *moving*."

"Yeah." I know.

"And it feels really good, you know? God. I feel so stupid."

"No! Why?"

"I know I shouldn't, but God, I should have stopped it. And it was so weird, he didn't even kiss me. And finally, after like forever, his hand starts, you know. Moving South? And finally I was like Jesus Christ I can't let him come all over my ass without even kissing me!"

"You said that?"

"No. I wish. I just turned around and looked at him again. And he just hugged me really hard. And then! He just rolled over and went to sleep."

"No!"

"Yes! God. I mean, we talked about it a bit this morning and stuff and I felt so dumb. He's not gonna tell his girl-friend, but I mean, how can I ever look at her again?"

"How can he?"

"I don't know."

"Jesus!"

"It's so weird. I've slept with, like, fifteen guys and it's one of my oldest friends who makes me feel like a whore."

"No! No." What else can I say? I scratch around my spaghetti pot of brains. What else can I say.

"Well. Anyway, I don't know. We have to go back in."

"Yeah."

Janet unties her apron and reties, tighter. I do the same. We go back in and seconds later we are auto-asking how we can help, what would you like?

Once Brian called me at work.

"Kinko's, how can I help you?"

"Hey, cockchocolate!" Such pride in his voice. "I've been

35

waiting all day to call you that!"

"It's beautiful."

It was. Only Brian had ever, *has* ever made me feel that I could, in fact, come anywhere near being chocolate to a cock. Oh, crassness! How shocking! But this is it. It's what I wanted. To be good-naturedly objectified, really, just a little. Made to feel worth my skin as a lady. And that's what he did. And the way he did it! Good Christ. First off, he took a queer theory course. And loved it! He made wonderful, witty, self-disparaging remarks about his own privilege all the time. And then! He would call me sugar! Gorgeous! Syrupy, hideous words like Beautiful. Babe. Sweetpea. Cockchocolate (it bears repeating).

Once he peed our initials into a gravel road, which remains the apogee of my romantic life.

But why? I wonder why. Why did these things make me, a girl with her head so tightly screwed on that it barely turned, all warm and buttery inside?

I ask Janet in the espresso corner.

"Buttery? What the fuck do you mean?"

My teeth click together, my tongue hangs around in my mouth like a mall rat.

It may be time to retire descriptives, unearth the soul and retire from language as it is known and spoken and written and woven to death.

On Thursday night Janet invites me to this bar called Casa del Popolo in an area of town that I've never seen, far from downtown, and much, much cooler. Janet and I arrive after work and join a tableful of her friends from school, including Lee of the bum grind. I give him a bored look when we're introduced but beam when I shake hands with Pierre, Martin, Frieda and Mylène. There's happy, poppy-but-not-mainstream music meandering through the place and the cute bartender serves us mini tumblers of wine, exciting vegetarian sandwiches and chips and salsa. Homemade! It reminds me a tiny bit of a place back home, which I don't dare mention, and I really dig it and everything would be absolutely perfect. If only I spoke French. Like everybody else. I feel like the most major asshole and I smile and nod like it's going out of style. Janet tries to switch everyone to English from time to time, but she invariably gets pulled back in by Martin or Mylène, especially as the night progresses and the wine does its job. To make matters worse, everyone is extremely friendly and continues to look at me as they speak, not realizing my almost total lack of comprehension. The interview for the Cup was one thing, but this is *Québécois* French at its quickest and most colloquial and I soon give up trying to add to the conversation with my chunky, boring sentences about how I have come from Toronto and am living in a small complex of apartments in the area of downtown. I feel like too much of a jerk to insistently speak English and I become content to let their conversation and laughter become a joyful burble in my brain as I look up at the embossed tin ceiling of the little bar, remembering the time I went to the doctor after Brian and I had started having sex. I told her I needed a prescription for birth control like it was no big deal, like I'd been having sex all my life. She asked me if I was in a monogamous relationship and I chirped, "Sure am!" One of my proudest moments. I have a gulp of wine and watch Janet laugh awkwardly with Lee. She follows him with her eyes as he goes to the washroom, her face wistful and confused.

"How's it going?" I ask her under my breath while he's gone.

"I can't hate him!" she whisper-yells in my ear, completely exasperated. She pushes in her wine-flushed cheeks with her hands and makes a growling noise. "I just don't want to act like a weirdo around everybody else. I don't want them to know."

I am at once completely flattered that I'm the only one she's told and kicked in the heart because this thing he's done isolates Janet from her friends. "I can try to hate him for you," I say.

"Thanks," says Janet just as Lee strides out of the bathroom, makes a lot of big hand gestures and says something loud and fast in French. Everyone laughs. Even the bartender. Lee's remarkably good looking. I squeeze Janet's hand under the table and she squeezes back. Hard.

"Regular size?"

"Yes please."

"With whipped cream?"

"A little."

Jowls forming under a fine face, a face with the dry leather look of middle-aged men, nice bone structure, a little bit *GQ*, a turtleneck. I hate turtlenecks. Glasses, tuft of gray hair. A little bit wild. This guy's in here all the time. Always "a little" whipped cream. For him I actually do it though. He usually tips.

Steaming the hot chocolate Janet tells me she thinks he's a babe.

"What? He's like forty-seven!"

"So?" She scoots past me to serve the Chai Latté. *Pshhhhhaaah* goes the steamer.

I give him the hot chocolate.

"Thanks."

The end.

The End.

Epilogue:

I am counting out my till at the end of the shift and he comes up to me and asks me if I write.

"Sometimes. How did you know?"

"You look for details."

Is this creepy? I paw around my insides looking for instinct. I'm coming up weirdly neutral. This must be a sign of either safety or an atrophied heart.

"I see the way you look at things. I've noticed what makes you smile some days. When people order skim milk hot chocolates with extra whipped cream for example. It always makes you smirk."

"It makes no sense!" I exclaim. I am exclaiming to this man. This man is smiling in this way that lets me know that I am an intelligent adult individual participating, nay, contributing to the intelligent adult individual world. He asks me if he could read something I've written and it just so happens that I have a little book with something folded and fraying in the back. A poem. And he practically snaps it from my fingers.

We agree to meet for coffee tomorrow, somewhere else, not my workplace, and he'll let me know what he thinks. He swishes out of the Cup in his gray, expensive pants and turtleneck.

"Nice work dude," says Janet, pretending to clean my table. She slow dances briefly with her gray plastic bussing bin.

"Seriously. It's not like that. He's telling me what he thinks of my poem. He knew I wrote. He said he could just tell."

"Who doesn't write?"

I know she's right. But I want to hold and cradle this being-called-special like I used to nurse that last sliver of Jolly Rancher in the corners of my rapacious mouth as long as I possibly could when I was a kid. Before it went back to the whole wheat and fruit snacks of sitting in my room thinking about Brian. Brian who thought I was special, too. Brian who told me in no uncertain terms that I was a good fucking writer.

Derek is a professor. Derek is divorced. Derek is forty-five. Derek teaches Middle English seminars. Derek speaks Latin. Derek has a lot of money. Derek likes to eat, go to plays and introduce me to people who run magazines who print poetry and promise me to send my manuscript to publishers as soon as its finished. I like to hang out with him, he motivates me to work hard, to send my stuff out and when I hang out with him I produce more than the dimly veiled erotica that I hunkered over in the room with the hanging plant during my time with Brian. Janet is convinced that I'm falling for him, that I'm having dreams of giving him head. I assure her I'm not that type of girl which makes us both laugh but I feel uncomfortable because there really *is* a type of girl to whom I refer, the kind who do fantasize about kneeling in front of father-aged cocks and looking into their owner's wise eyes from miles below. Not me! He's just helping me get what I want: my fight back.

Over sushi, the kind with salmon eggs in it that pop and spurt goopy in my mouth, I tell Derek of my pain.

"He just. I just feel fucking shucked, you know? Like oysters."

"I got it."

"Yeah. I just. I can't even describe it."

"That's love."

"Yeah. But it's gone!"

He puts his hand on mine and he looks at me and he smiles and his face looks warm and I pop a salty fish egg between my front teeth.

"It's going to take a long time," he says. "You need to let love come out of you. You need to let it come out slow and steady so that it doesn't stick forever. Does that make sense?"

It does. It does? It does it does it does.

I dissolve a whack of wasabi on my tongue and let it burn and try to let the love leak out with Derek's big strong hand holding. Holding.

"I think you could really use some body work," Derek says. We're at the Musée d'art contemporain, looking at large, sloppy paintings of breasts and fish. "All this emotional stress you're experiencing lately. It's taking its toll on your body."

"Thanks a lot," I say to him in a hushy art gallery voice. I'm being sarcastic but I try to straighten my back a little nevertheless.

"Don't get me wrong," Derek says and his warm eyes twinkle. "You look absolutely great, don't worry. It's just that it's obvious you're carrying things with you. You see, I'm learning this method, it's called rolfing—"

"Sounds really appealing."

"I know, great name. But it works, I've been rolfed, so to speak, when I lived out in California, that's where it got started. Anyway, it made an amazing difference to my posture, I felt thirty pounds lighter."

"Hm," I say.

"This was around the time of my divorce, you know, and I was trying to do everything in my power to bounce back, eating well, swimming, yoga, the whole bit. But I still felt just zonked, all the time. I mean not just emotionally. Physically, too."

"Yeah?" I have been feeling hunchier lately. We're walking slowly past the paintings, making a requisite pause in front of each canvas.

"I was an absolute wreck. So I went to this bodywork clinic, thinking maybe I'd wrenched something at the gym. And they rolfed me. Let me tell you, it wasn't just physical. Not by any means. It really proved the mind/body connection to me in a more tangible way than I've ever experienced. It just takes you places you've never been. I cried when it was over, I'm not kidding. I hadn't cried in years."

"Because it hurt so much?" I don't know why I'm so quippy and lame sometimes, but Derek doesn't seem to mind.

"It does hurt sometimes, yes, it's really deep tissue manipulation, that's why it works. It actually focuses on the connective tissue rather than on the muscles."

"Neat."

"So I've been learning it here in Montreal, hoping to help people in my old age. I figure it'll be something worthwhile to do with my retirement. I bring it up only because I think it could really benefit you considering everything you've been going through. I mean, just if you ever feel you want to of course."

"Yeah, maybe. I guess I have been a little run down."

"It's understandable. Love is a huge thing to lose," says Derek and touches my shoulder. "Let's go in here," he says, tightening his grip on my shoulder and steering me away from the paintings.

"Oh, but isn't there another room of these?" I ask. "I like them."

"You'll *love* this," he says and propels me into an installation room. Of course he's already seen the exhibit twice. The room has a TV set in the middle and nothing else. I look around, waiting for the punchline.

"What? Where is it?" I say. About forty seconds later I say it again. But it's not *me* me, it's me on TV. It taped me looking around like a forlorn idiot and it taped Derek standing next to me, chuckling. "Aw man, that's awesome!" I say.

"You don't think it's invasive?" Derek asks.

I think for a minute. Then I say, "Most good art is inva-

43

sive." Why do I say such dumb shit?

Derek thinks then. About what I've said. "You're really smart, you know that?"

"Thanks," I say, pink-faced, and we carry on.

Derek assures me that what's important now is the cultivation of my talent my talent my talent the word stoppers all the raw, woundy bits in my head and my heart that Brian made there, stoppers them like cotton wool. I know they're still suppurating sores, I haven't lost touch completely, but I am sure that this is aiding the healing process, and before I know it Derek has booked me to read at Blizzarts on Boulevard St. Laurent on a Friday night.

Walking in with Derek means that I have to meet fourteen people per minute and be witty and charming with each one. I'm draped in a gauzy fabric. I'm not wearing a bra. Janet said it would be best. She said nobody cares nipples any more. I have to admit: I care nipples. Attempting to be breezy and carefree I touch a woman's elbow when we're introduced. She stares at the elbow. Then at me. Then her mouth cracks into something harsh and unpleasant and she stares at me and then she says it!

"Did you just touch my elbow?"

"Yeah."

"That's really interesting." Something like a smile follows. Then she's gone. Jesus! Touching this woman's elbow is probably, of all of the things I've ever done in my life, probably the least interesting.

"Easy crowd I guess," I say, completely to myself but Derek hears me and laughs.

Wait though! He couldn't have gotten my joke. It had an internal punchline. Are we that in sync? He's steering me toward a plasticky table with some cheap looking chairs that probably have street-cred.

"So when are you quitting the Cup?" he says once we've sat down with a little Ikea candle between us whose flame flickers in our sweaty glasses of rye. This is something he says a lot lately. He suggests that I could do a lot better than the Cup. That I don't need that in my life. That I'm too talented.

"What's wrong with the Cup?" I say which is what I always say. "I'd miss Janet."

"Why don't you take my course?"

"I don't want to be in school right now. Remember? I came here to do different stuff. To figure out what I want to do."

"You came here to lose Brian. Brian's lost."

"Thanks."

"Hey." Derek has a hand on my face. I hate when this happens because it means that my face has fallen just that little bit too far. It means that I'm not over it after all. That the talentwool stuffed into my wounds is becoming supersaturated One More Time in gummy regret. And nostalgia. And reeling jealousy. But Derek looks at me with his assurance eyes.

"It'll just take time. Trust me."

I do. He must know! A divorcé for Christ's sake.

"I'll think about doing a course anyway. But I don't know if I want to take yours. That would be kind of weird."

"Oh come on."

I sip my rye and ginger and start to get the same grating I get in my belly every time I think about Amber from work.

Only this time it's because I'm about to read a poem in front of the entire literati scene of Concordia University in a den of dive-chic with a whirring air conditioner and a single mic set up. For the likes of me! I look at Derek and want to feel something other than cold appreciation. Then I doublethink myself a reminder that that's all I should feel anyway since we both know our relationship is strictly professional with a slight paternal feeling on the part of the patriarch.

I drink. Too much.

Three drinks before I go up.

I make jokes.

"So, you guys like my nipples?" Ha. I read: two poems. Wait.

clap. clap. clap. clap. clap.clap.clap. clap.

I tripped over at least eleven words. I tripped over the word "so".

I stumble on my way back to my table and some guy leaning against the wall laughs at me.

Before I know what's happening something large and bulky zips past me. I stop in my tracks. It's Derek. He's suddenly about half a centimeter away from the laugher's face.

"You better shut the fuck up before I give you a piece of my mind," Derek hisses. His eyes look as hard as little wet stones. I've never seen them that way before.

"Hey, hey. Buddy. Calm down," the laugher says, backing away. "I wasn't even laughing at your girl, okay, it was something else. Just calm the fuck down."

They keep staring at each other. This is weird. I want to leave. I take a step away from where I've been rooted for the past minute.

"Derek can we go now?"

Too loud.

Derek huffs and turns from the guy. "Take my arm," he says, offering it. I take it and he leads me out the door.

I cry in the parking lot. Too much. He hugs me. Too much. I say okay when he says we should go back to his place and eat some pizza and maybe watch a movie and forget about writing for a little.

"The poems are really good. You know I think so," Derek says in the cab.

"I know. I know."

"They liked it. That little jerk in front didn't know his ass from his elbow."

"I know. I know."

We get to his house and I know it should be weird because we've never hung out at his house before but it doesn't feel weird. It just feels like another event that he's treating me to. Just like the theatre or the art exhibits we've gone to. Mired in the aftermath of my own mediocrity at Blizzarts I forgot to pay attention to where the cab was taking us. We could be anywhere.

The place, not weirdly, is big and beautiful. There are big exposed beams on the vaulted ceilings and there are high gloss hard wood floors and a record player and bookshelves bookshelves everywhere. The kitchen appliances are made out of brushed aluminum and there seems to be a smell piped in from somewhere that is like camping and Fall.

I go into the bathroom—painted orange—and Derek goes to the kitchen to put a pizza in the oven. I am comforted that he's getting the pizza out of the freezer. Like a normal person. This is normal.

I come out of the bathroom looking, I'm sure, dejected as all hell. Fuck I miss Brian. Why don't you materialize and tell me I'm wonderful and brush my hair out of my face and smile at me with your small eyes? *You have small eyes!* What other girl would ever even like you?

"Jesus, when will it *end?*" I yell, slumping down on Derek's low couch. I'm yelling at myself, but of course Derek's here, too.

"Are you okay?" he asks, from the doorway of the kitchen.

"Yeah."

"Are you sure?"

"Yeah. I'm just really, really. I don't know. The thing just went so badly, and I just miss… Hey listen," I say suddenly. I've had an idea. "Remember that thing you were telling me about last week? That ralfing thing or whatever?"

"Rolfing."

"Do you think maybe you could. I don't know. Maybe give it a try?"

Derek pauses, thinking it over, and suddenly I want him to do this more than anything in the world, I want something new, something healing, I want to feel.

"Sure," he says finally. "Yeah. If you're up for it I think it might be a really good time to try it. We could do just a mini-session. While the pizza bakes."

"Will it help?"

"I can almost guarantee it."

In the bedroom of a forty-five year old man there are pictures of that man in Greece and Nepal and there are masks on the walls from Africa and there is a bedspread and a lot of pillows.

"Why don't you take off your top?"

"What?"

"I need to see the back to do it properly."

"No, maybe not then."

"Oh come on." Just like he said when I said it would be weird to take his course.

"Oh come on. You think I haven't seen everything before? It's not a big deal." He steps toward me and takes both of my hands. "This is sacred work, Kate. The first thing is trust."

He's right. Who cares. I'm sure he's seen a bra before. Good thing I didn't wear one! Gauzy fabric. I'm being a prude and a baby and I'm lying down on the bed, my top folded in the corner of the bedroom of a forty-five year old man. I lie on my front so all you can see is my back. My supple, apricot back. Who said that?

Derek comes back in from the living room where he has tastefully been doing nothing but exercising good taste, allowing me to take my top off at my own leisure, giving me every reason to trust him. And I do. I am grateful to him. For his presence in my life. I *don't* need the Cup. I'm better than that. They liked the poem! They did. Derek said. They were just a tough crowd. Maybe I should have stuck with elbow-touching.

He starts to poke and prod and rub my shoulders, my back. He tells me the tissue feels really tight, it's good that

I'm doing this. He starts to push harder, it even hurts a bit, but I don't mind because it's also warm, really really warm and I can feel something moving, something I thought was just in my head but it's not. Things become locked in our bodies and as much as I thought that was nice and poetic and just the right thing for a young woman's mentor to say in an even, convincing tone over sushi, I didn't really believe it until now. Now that he's unlocking things in me with his hands. My muscles, holding fast to Brian, going further down, hugging onto any time my father told me I could look nicer or people in highschool asking, "Are you a boy or a girl?" Such a typical, typical suburban upbringing, a good one, and still, still there it is in the body, glommed onto with all its own might: Pain. And I'm crying and I have no real idea why it's all just melting into fluids and it's coming out of me like it needs to come out and I think that maybe just maybe just maybe after this I won't think about it any more. I'll write it all down and read it all out and there will be standing ovations and it will be done. Maybe the nightmares of Amber from work will be gone, maybe I won't feel the scratch of Brian's stubble, the hushed breath of his whisper, "you're so good" condensing on my ear in my sickening waking dreams maybe it will all melt. Away.

I'm crying audibly. Loudly even. I feel his hands but not really. I see the bed but not really. I hear him say, "You've been hurt." I feel his hands turn me over. I feel his hands. But not really. But not really. And I don't come out of it until.

I can't believe it.

He's going down on me.

It's so embarrassing.

He's going down on me.
Is there no better way to say this?
He's going down on me.
He's going down on me.
And I freeze.

He kisses me on the mouth. Frozen. Solid.

He looks down at me and smiles. But his eyes. Cold. Wet. Stones. What now? Oh God, what now? He looks down at me, he smiles, the door is locked, we're alone, his eyes are cold, and all that I feel is fear and the only word I hear is rape. He could rape me. All the tacit, lifelong anxiety that I've gone through life with, that it could happen to me, like cancer or a car crash, was not even close to being enough preparation for this moment.

I feebly try to smile back up at him, try to make my eyes say that everything's okay, that I'm still having a wonderful time, that there's no reason to be angry, no reason at all.

Finally he turns away. "I can see our session is done for the day," he says and gets up off the bed. He hands me a silk robe. Beautiful. There is no question in my mind that it was bought directly from a real live kimono-wearing Geisha girl in Japan. Probably for his wife. I say nothing. I put it on. I feel so stupid. What the hell is wrong with me? Why am I here? I don't have the right to say anything. I offered him my trust. He only did what he thought was... It's not true. I'm not even thinking this. I'm not thinking anything. Maybe, "This robe is cool."

Suddenly Derek's face lights up, a bulldozer of fear plows right through me and the thinking starts again. No one even knows I'm here and he goes over to his outsized oak dresser and opens a drawer and pulls out a box. He hands it to me, I open it and there, staring up at me is a hideous, gnarled hand wrought out of pewter and strung on a silver chain.

"It's the glove Criseyde gave Troilus as a symbol of her love," he says smiling.

"Oh." I don't remember who they are. Did Troilus kill Criseyde?

"I got it when I was travelling in Scotland. This tiny medievalist shop in the Orkneys."

"Wow."

I hold my breath as he fastens it around my neck and I follow when he leads me to the vast, orange bathroom. We stand in front of the mirror together and he puts his hands on my shoulders. I try not to jump.

"Look at that," he says. "You're beautiful."

I look at us standing there, me pale and small with this ugly love-glove around my neck, Derek nodding serenely. I want out I want out now I want out so badly but what if his serenity snaps like it did with the laugher and this thought scares my face into what I hope will pass for a grateful smile.

We sit in the living room and eat the pizza. It's good. *The pizza's good.* Derek puts on a movie. *Quest for Fire.* Grunting. Grunting. He sees my unshaven legs poking out from the robe.

"You're like a little furry animal," he says and ruffles my hair. Like I'm thirteen.

Grunt grunt goes the movie.

"I have to phone Janet," I say. "I said I'd call her after the reading. I forgot."

Beep beep beep boop beep boop boop.

"Janet? Oh! Right. I will. I'll be right there! No. Sorry. I forgot. No. No. No."

Janet: "Hi! What's up? Hello? Are you okay? Where are you?"

"Derek, I have to go. Janet is waiting for me. She didn't go out because she was waiting for me to call. I'm sorry."

"No problem. Call you tomorrow?"

A little smile, collecting my top, staring at my feet on my way out the door. Ha ha ha ha ha ha ha ha hahahaha-hawhore!

Careening through the streets of Old Montreal, because that's where we are (who knew?), my sobs echo off cobble stones, my gauzy top gets soaked with rain. Who cares nipples any more? Ain't that the truth. Cab! Cab! I'm yelling recklessly trying to stanch my tears with rage. Trying to make anger come. I didn't get into the cab that Derek called for me, told the driver I'm happy to walk in the same dull waxy voice in which I thanked Derek for the pizza and the opportunity to read tonight.

I get home and feel sick. There is no other word for it. I am disgusted, revolted with myself, how could I ever have let this happen? He bought me dinners for Christ's sake, he took me to a play. People don't just do those things, I am a grown woman, I am twenty-one years old, this is something I should know. There was a little voice OF COURSE there was a little voice that whispered the whole time that he might be sleazy, your writing's really not that good, no one would do this much for you if they didn't expect. Something. And I just didn't listen. I outright refused to listen and why? Because that's how bad I wanted the attention, because that's how good it felt to be told that I'm somebody again, because I wanted "something new" (and I quote my own feeble self). Pathetic! Completely and utterly pathetic. I've already had two showers but it just won't go away.

I sit in my bed but I can't lie down because every time I do I feel his hands again and I'm scared. I'm scared that he'll call tomorrow, I'm scared that he'll want to see me and I hate him, I hate him I'm so scared of his eyes and his hands and of this body they touched and of this crazy crazy brain that I don't even know any more. I have to tell someone right now because I can't sleep and I'm digging my nails into my legs. I know I should phone Janet, I know I should, I do, but I'm crying and I'm scared and I'm shivering and I'm cold and there is only one voice that I want to hear and only one person I want to tell.

I phone Brian.

Oh! Don't groan.

I don't need him as a boyfriend, I just need him as a friend. A guy pal? A male perspective?

Come on. Don't groan.

I just need somebody who knows me right now, I just need a familiar voice and whether you believe me or not, whether *I* believe me or not is at this juncture irrelevant because I'm gonna go ahead and do it anyway... here we go.

"Hi, Brian?"

Nothing.

"Brian. Look, don't worry I'm not calling you to do any of the stuff I did last time. I'm really sorry about that anyway. I shouldn't have done that. I was just calling to see how you were. As a friend. Really."

"Kate. It's two in the morning." It's his just-woke-up voice.

"I know. I'm sorry. I'm really sorry."

"Hey, are you okay?"

"Yeah. I. I think so. Um. Brian? We've known each other long enough now to tell each other everything right?"

"Sure. I guess. Of course. Of course we have. What's up?"

"Well. I… um, I've been hanging out with this guy here for the last couple of weeks, this, um, older guy and he was, like, helping me get my writing off the ground and stuff and tonight I did this reading at this bar—"

"Hey, that's awesome!"

"Yeah. Thanks. So anyway, then he sort of took me home and I was feeling really depressed and stuff and then he was giving me this massage and like. Things got really intense, like I didn't even know where I was, Brian, I swear to God, it was the weirdest thing, it was like I was in this trance or something, it's this really weird kind of massage technique or something and anyway, once I finally, like, came out of it, he was. He was going down on me." It's really true, that's how I said it. This is no word of a lie. This is direct transcription. No build up, no breeze-shooting, no nothing.

"What? Dude! Are you serious?"

I realize that in print the response "dude" appears almost categorically inappropriate, but I can assure you it was flung forth so sincerely and with such intensity that it was impossible to fault. I. Hate. To. Say. This (But if it's going to be said it might as well be overwritten): I bask in the warmth of the concern I've caused, the panic I've stirred. I'm also crying suddenly, uncontrollably. I tell him all of it. The sushi. The art gallery. The rolfing. Everything. I hear Toronto air suck into Brian hard and fast, so many miles away. He is pissed off.

"I swear to God, Kate, that guy is fucking dead, that is disgusting."

"But I just feel so stupid, I mean, how could I have let it come to this?"

"What? Come on Kate, you didn't let it come to anything! The guy's a fuckin perve."

"Yeah I know, but—"

"But nothing! But nothing. Katy. Jesus, this was not your fault, he fucking assaulted you. That makes me so mad, that sick bastard, I swear to God. If I was there right now I'd rip his old man arms off." And I know that if he was here right now he wouldn't do a damn thing because he's a small, skinny man but he would rage like this and I could watch his eyes.

We keep talking for awhile and I tell him how scared I am and by the end of it all Brian has called me baby. Once. We're murmuring to each other. It's definitely murmuring. Murmuring is what lovers do!

"I am so sorry. I really am. That asshole. That makes me want to rip shit up."

"Thank you."

"Are you okay?"

"I think so. Thank you."

"I'll call you soon, okay?"

"Uh huh. Thanks, Brian."

"Take care."

"Bye."

Gone. Have you ever actually taken your pillow and really really truly imagined that it had the face of your estranged beloved? Held it against you and nestled your cheek against its downy softness? Used your own arm and your hobbled, deranged imagination to put "his" arm around you, to pull you close? Maybe even kissed that well worn cotton casing? Just a little kiss?

Yeah. Neither have I.

Janet and I sit in Westmount Park. Westmount is the area of Montreal where the wealthy Anglos live. So I've been told. When you walk into Westmount the streetlamps change. It's true. I've wondered about this many times. Who paid for them? They have old fashioned, kind of wrought-irony looking casings and the light that comes out of them! Well. You walk around in Westmount come dusk and you are on a soundstage. For the type of movie set in times gone by, times when light was still soft and romance a whimsical happy thing you could romp after and eventually snare to tickle and wrestle with in your lovely feather bed all night. In Westmount the birds will chirp in the morning. There will be no gull-squack. Because of those lights! Who pays? Did the people of Westmount have a meeting and decide in hard fast English that this would be a worthwhile purchase? Did everybody chip in twenty bucks? Per month? Per day?

Peeling pieces off a blade of grass I try to talk about this.

Like so much gloopy mortar. The heaviness sits around.

"This has got to stop," Janet says suddenly, and looks right at me.

"What?"

"You're avoiding the issue, you're being mopey, I don't know what the hell Brian said to you last night——" I made the mistake of telling her I phoned him. Now she says "Brian" the way most people say Hitler.

"Brian told me he wanted to beat the fuck out of him."

"Oh that's just terrific, that's just what you need. Is he gonna pee on you while he's at it? Mark his territory? Jesus, this is what I'm saying, we need to get you out of this, you need to open your eyes!"

"I know, I mean. I guess he overreacted a bit, but——"

"No, he did not overreact, Derek is a gross old dude, someone *should* beat the fuck out of him, but that someone should be you, do you see what I'm saying? You don't need Brian to get mad for you."

"How can I get mad though, Janet? I played right into his whole thing. I mean, just because I didn't know what the hell was going on, that's not really his fault is it. For Christ's sake, I'm the one who asked for the massage!"

"You did?"

"Yeah." This is the first time I've said it out loud and I want to stick my head in the ground.

"Oh dude."

"I know!"

We sit in silence for about thirty seconds and I listen to the shrieks of kids on the playground. Now Janet will tell me what I already know: what the hell did I expect?

"You know that is just sad."

Harsh. "I know Janet, I know, I mean, in retrospect it seems completely—"

"Not you. Him. That's just so low. I mean, you must have really been feeling shitty that night if you asked for a massage. I mean, I know you. You don't even usually like it when people at work hug you. And what better time to get at an unsuspecting young lady's lady parts than when she's feeling like shit?"

A little girl laughs a cackly little girl laugh from somewhere nearby and I can't help but get the creeps. "But. What if I asked for a massage because I was ready to get it on? I wasn't. But how would he know that?"

"Come on. If he thought that, do you think he would have bothered with the whole massage preamble? Why do you think he told you all that shit about him being a body artist or whatever the hell he is?"

"Oh come on. He's not—"

"That gross? Oh yes he is. This is what I'm saying, Kate."

Is it possible that she's right? "I don't get it. I don't even know what happened. I just know that I'm really freaked out. I mean, he said he'd call me today. What if he just doesn't get that I don't want to see him?"

"Return the necklace." A classic beer-case-on-a-counter statement.

I take a breath of muggy, parky air. "Okay," I say. "But what if he just really didn't know he was crossing the line?"

"So? Do you really feel like hanging out with Creepy McGee after this?"

"No!" I would rather cut my gums open with a nail file.

"But what about Lee? You stayed friends with him."

"That's different." She pauses for a minute. Her face contorts. She shakes her little arms in front of her like an angry muppet.

"Yeah. It's different. But still."

We sit there still, in the still, soft, richpeople light.

We put the necklace in a baggie that afternoon and tie it up and Janet slinks up the stairs of his building while I wait on the corner of his cobblestone street. She puts the baggie on his doorstep and we go back downtown and I hug her and go home. I feel scared, but glad that I don't have to see that ugly thing any more and glad that he'll at least get the hint.

He calls two hours later. I let it go to the machine.

"Kate. I am insulted. I can't believe that you would react this way, I thought you were far more mature than that," his voice is even, normal as fries. "The sexual attraction I felt for you was in the moment. I thought it was clear that you felt the same way. If I was mistaken, I apologize, but I am truly disappointed in this rash, childish reaction. I think you have a lot more growing up to do than I thought you did."

He hangs up and I stand alone in my tiny apartment, wracked with fear, with disgust, with relief, with confusion, my head and body yanked apart, myself lost somewhere in the shuffle.

How is it possible that things have become so heavily plot-based in such a short period of time? I envisioned my life in Montreal as a novel-length stack of vignettes, witty observances, aphoristic glances at life after love. I moved here for something new, yes, but I don't think I actually wanted anything to *happen*. And now the whole goddamn love-ball has followed me here, rolling through Montreal and sucking things in, seething, growing, it won't let me hit the brakes, just drives its massive, overflowing monster-truckload of rancid, aging garbage straight at me all day and if I don't keep running with it, grabbing at bits of debris, putting them places, toiling away to shelve chunks of this fecund mess, it will overflow and bury me and run me right down. I can't stop I can't take the makeup off I can't stop not for a second because if I do.

I'm nothing.

It's true. Nothing. *I* am all I have now and *this* is all I am and I used to be so very much more and it really takes some getting used to.

Take my status as a girl for example. I used to feel like one all the time. A real live one. A pretty one even some days, like the cockchocolate day, for example. Or sometimes, when Brian woke up, he would run his hands along the length of my body until my eyes fluttered open and he'd be looking at me, smiling.

"I love your girlbumps," he said once.

But now he doesn't. I know this happens all the time, but it makes you think, doesn't it? You wind up thinking this new girl, let's call her, um, Amber, this Amber is more girl than you, don't you? You wind up wondering what's wrong with ME that I couldn't please him? What's lacking in me? Is my body not woman enough? Is my mind not woman enough, is my very SOUL not woman enough? And we're not talking, you know, nailpolish and underwire bras here either. We're talking the very social fabric of girlness. Gone with Brian. What happens? Crazy. Barf in the shower.

So you try to do something about it, you try to reinvent yourself, construct yourself a shiny new subjectivity, like, let's say "artist" since the whole "girl" thing didn't work out. Let some older, mentor type talk you up, like you can write, like you have a brain, like "you notice details don't you?" And, drumroll please:

Receive creepy, unsolicited cunnilingus. Tadaaaaaa!

Repeat process.

Repeat process.

REPEAT PROCESS?

I'm sorry, I didn't mean to get weird on you, please stay with me. Please. Stay with me. You are all I have.

For the next three weeks I have nightmares of the reading and Derek and his bedroom and the pizza and his hands and sometimes I wake up with a sweaty shivery feeling in my spine. I spend the days at the Cup staring out the wall-sized windows, worried that he'll come in. My milk-foaming speed goes down the tubes, Isabelle catches me adding too much syrup to my Corettos twice. When I walk home, my heart always beats faster when I get to my intersection, afraid that his car will be waiting at the corner where we used to meet, that he'll pull me in. Thank God he doesn't know which building is mine.

As much as Janet tells me it's not my fault, that Derek's scum, I feel stupid all the time and my performance at work conveniently corroborates this opinion. I know it's my fault, at least a bit, and it looks like Brian's figured that out too since he certainly hasn't called to see how I'm doing even though he said he'd call soon. Maybe after his moment of rash anger he's thought this one through and is busy telling Amber how his ex has gone off the deep-end, has become a slut, is giving it up to any guy who looks her way, I mean why else would he not have called if he said he'd call soon?

Not that I should be surprised, he used to do this all the time. "Soon" was among his favourite words. When we were first dating, last spring, before we lived together, he would always call me "soon".

I remember a few five or even six day periods spent waiting for "soon" to arrive, enjoying the independence for the first day or three, hanging out with friends on the fourth, then settling in for the fifth or sixth, Bob Dylan at the ready, nursing a bowl of peanut butter and chocolate ice cream, steeling myself for our imminent, messy break-up. At this point I've cut the crap and eat straight from the tub, the sodden cardboard bottom cold and wet in my lap. Then as now the phone's rude, dorky jangle gives me half a heart attack and I'm almost annoyed to have my mope interrupted.

"Katy! How are ya?"

The cheap barbs of bliss that work through my body at the sound of Brian's voice—a voice that is smooth like coffee and chocolate—prevent me from salvaging any semblance of dignity. He has called, I am sold.

"What's up?" I say. At least I sound guarded. At least I sound tough.

"Nothing. Just calling to say hi."

"Well, hi," I say.

There is some silence here and I think he must be figuring out the phrasing to ask me how I'm doing, if I'm okay.

"So how's Montreal?" he asks.

"Well, okay."

"Just okay?"

Jesus Christ, Brian! Did he just forget? "Yeah, just okay," I say, a tiny sliver of sarcasm sliding in, expanding. "I mean, I guess it would be better if I wasn't living in constant fear of running into my molester."

"Oh shit, yeah!" he says. "Every time I think about that I get so fucking mad."

"Yeah. Well, me too."

"So what else is new?"

"Nothing, Brian. That was kind of a big deal. Other than that, I work. Really, that's it." I'm being almost cold! I'm impressing myself.

"Shit," he says. "My bagel's burning. Can you hold on?"

"Of course." I hold on. I realize I am gripping the receiver so hard I'm sweating, my ear is warm and red. I concentrate on loosening my grip.

"Okay, I'm back," he says.

"Hi."

There is a wait. A big wait.

"Kate."

"Yeah?"

"I really miss you. I want to be friends. I. I really still consider you my best friend."

"Yeah?" Those little electric barbs of bliss poke, jolt, pierce, buzz, but I'm fighting back. "Brian, why did you wait so long to call me?"

"I didn't."

"Brian. It's been three weeks. I told you something big."

"I'm sorry. I. I didn't want to push things."

"Whatever." Man, I'm cooking with gas here.

"I guess I just didn't realize how much the whole thing fucked you up."

"Yeah. It kind of did."

"I'm sorry," he says. "I know I'm fucking up. But I really want us to be friends. Really. I just. No one gets me like you do."

I'm gripping the receiver again, I catch myself in the mirror, checking if I look okay. How can he be so good at this? Then I remember something.

"What about Amber?" I spit her name out like it's a razor blade in my Hallowe'en candy.

"No. Not in the same way. I miss talking to you."

"Are you still with her?"

"Yeah."

I look at my face in the mirror, eyes swollen and red, my forehead wrinkled up, I feel my hot ear against the phone, the cut of the bliss barbs, the knot of biley hell called Amber that has stalked my stomach for the last month and a half and it's only then that my brain registers what my larynx did: "No."

"Okay," he sounds truly stricken.

"Not now, Brian. I can't. I'm sorry."

"It's okay."

"I don't think we should talk for a little while." Can you believe this? I am good!

"Yeah. I. I understand. Um. I just."

"I know."

Another wait. But littler.

"I have to go, Brian."

"Yeah. Call me when you want to. Please. I would love to hear from you."

"I will."

Cah-Lick!

Hoo hah! Yes! One point for the good guys. I start crying but it feels good. Still crying most of the night, sifting through photos, smelling old t-shirts with the Dylan on. It Ain't Me Babe. No no no. Still crying when Janet calls but just busting with pride when I tell her what happened.

"That's great."

"That's not just great, Janet," I sniffle wetly. "That's a small fucking miracle!"

I have decided to join the YMCA. It seems like the right thing to do. There are one billion, I mean it, one billion articles written about how exercise is a good way to battle depression, lethargy, to get your mind off things, fight PMS, memorize things better, get more sleep, prevent breast cancer, stave off acne, improve sexual performance I mean the more you read about it the more you start to wonder how it's even possible that you're not already dead, and signing the pre-authorized payment form for fifty bucks a month to the brand new Stanley Street Y feels as good as a shot of wheatgrass and an echinacea pie.

When I get home from my grand tour of the facilities, my first Step Toning for Beginners class, and an invigorating shower in the sprawling, sparkling changeroom, I decide that it's high time I cleaned up my apartment. I scour and sweep and dust and wash and get a load of laundry on the go. It's revolting how much dirt has settled around me in the past two months. "I haven't seen Brian for two whole months," I say out loud as I go out my back door, onto the fire escape landing to shake out my yellow rug. There's a girl a meter away from me, on the adjacent landing. She looks up at me and I feel like a dolt for talking to myself. I've seen her going into the building before, and have admired her amazing posture and long, black hair. Now she's squatting, straight-backed, holding a peanut out to a brash, bony squirrel who arrogantly grabs the offering and takes off down the stairs.

"Aw, he touched me with his little claws!" says the girl and smiles at me.

I suppress my rabies paranoia and smile back. "Cute," I say.

"I know. I've been trying to feed that one for awhile now, and he finally took something." She's gotten up and is leaning against the railing of her fire escape.

"How do you know it's the same one?" I ask, but her answer is cut off by a ridiculously loud door slam.

"Fucking Christly hell!" comes booming into the hot afternoon from the angry old man's apartment. He lives three doors down from the black-haired girl. "Goddamn fucking assholes fucking rip me off every goddamn fucking time, fucking chicken frying sons of bitches."

"I gotta go inside," says the girl. "I can't take this shit any more. I have to wear headphones till he shuts the hell up."

I give her a knowing smile and let go of a corner of my rug to wave. She locks herself back into her place and I start beating my rug against the railings.

"Swear to God, they're the fucking chickens. Fucking chickens. Snap their chicken bones. Fuck."

The dust billows out of my rug and into the humid air between the buildings. It hangs in a cloud with the old man's conflagration of filth that continues to smoke long after I, too, have retreated into my apartment. I sit on my couch, flip through a *Cosmo* and listen to my Walkman. A mix tape that Brian made me in the early days. A half-nagging, half-calming voice in my head repeatedly reminds me that everything is going great.

"Baby. Tony died. I'm really sorry."

It's my mother on the phone.

Tony is the guinea pig.

We've had him six years.

My mom is crying.

"His hair just started falling out and I took him to the vet, but she said it was just too late. She said that it was his time."

I remember Brian holding Tony on his lap one time. Squeaking together. They had just met each other. Brian looked so awed and intimidated, Tony looked so happy and fat. What did I think? "That's how he'll look at our baby." Christ almighty.

"I'm sorry, Mommy. I really am."

Tony was not just any guinea pig. He filled the void in our family life that usually takes a whole dog to fill. He was a free-range pig and when, rarely, this caused too much of a ruckus he was confined to a kiddy pool that took up a good quarter of the family room. He used a litter box, we brushed him weekly with a toothbrush, he was fat and had kind of a bitchy personality and he was among the best friends I've ever had. My father fed him his own teacup of porridge every morning.

Janet takes my weekend shifts and I take a train to Toronto for the first time in two and a half months. I'm going to the funeral.

In Toronto I cry with my family and we eat our cabbage rolls in appreciative silence, thinking of Tony in his backyard grave. My parents go to bed at tennish and I'm left alone in the house in the suburbs. You may have already noticed my startling lack of connection to anyone back in Toronto. It's true. I'm one of those girls who got so into her boyfriend that I required no more than a few close friends, plus a handful of acquaintances, people to invite to a party, people to whom I could serve a devilled egg. My best friend, Sabrina, is travelling in India for a year and anyone else I might want to talk to is busy barrelling through university in London, Guelph, Kingston, Waterloo, the Torontonian post-highschool diaspora.

I watch TV, I sit around, I try to read, the house hums and whirs and I'm jealous of my parents sharing a warm bed, sharing a warm sleep. Pop music on MuchMusic Janet in my head, "Whatever you do don't go see Brian when you're in Toronto." *Whatever you do.* Pop music on MuchMusic I just can't get you out of my head. Boy your lovin's all I think about. I just can't get you out of my head. Boy it's more than I care to think about.

The next evening my dad is golfing, my mom's having a nap. I borrow the car, leave a note *Back in a bit*. I head downtown. I take the QEW in from Mississauga and feel the future all around me. Lights blooping and blinking, billboards moving and talking, the CN Tower a silly little lighthouse humoured for old time's sake.

I'm on my way to see Brian. I was sneaky about it, I'm sorry. It happened between this section and the previous, in the space-break as the pro writers call it. I called Brian in the space-break. I guess I didn't want you to see. Janet told me not to after all, and my parents would kill me. I think my mom was secretly pleased when I sobbed my cuckold status into the phone two months ago because it had meant that our breakup would stick and she wouldn't have to hear about Brian Johnson any more. But we're just having one drink. It can't hurt. I'll be right back. I promise.

We've agreed to meet at Union Station, then go to the bar on top of the CN Tower. It's something we liked to do sometimes, to be fancy, to be silly but *I* didn't suggest we do it tonight, I mean I'm not crazy, I'm not trying to re-live old times here, it was his suggestion, not mine, I just want to talk to him, you know, I'm feeling awfully self-conscious here, awfully judged, awfully LOOK. I know it appears that I'm probably doing the worst thing I could ever possibly do here, having come such a long way, having abstained from being his friend for a full eleven days, but look, I know what I'm doing and the thing that no one seems to understand, that Janet can't possibly understand, that no one could ever understand is just what good friends we were. How much fun we had together. I just want to talk to him. That's all. Really. Okay. Can I continue? Can I?

He's late, which is no surprise, he's always late. I've got a nervous tummy but it's kind of fun. I mean, we haven't seen each other in months. Maybe he's got new facial hair. He probably looks terrible and it's just making me smile, the idea of Brian with some greasy new pompadour that Amber encourages, or a neck beard or something when he comes around the corner THWACKboom. That would be the sound of my whole mass of pounding insides, you know, heart, stomach, probably liver and kidneys too just pounding THWACK ripping right through my body, out of my skin, right out into the open, trying, straining to get a better look and then boom, retreating back into my middle where they're supposed to be but all shivering and quaking and whispering amongst themselves because damn. He just looks so good. Keep it together Kate. But I have never, never seen a man before or since wear used cords and an old t-shirt with quite that much verve and personality and Jesus, there's this video montage tearing through my brain of me undoing those cords, pulling the zipper down, pulling the old t-shirt up over his head, his breath hot on my face and his hands pulling at strings and zippers and stuff on me and there he is, the real thing, The Guy, Brian superimposed over everything, walking, it seems like slow motion, smiling across the brown tiles of the station, past the ice cream store, the newsstand and now he's here. Holy shit. This was not part of the plan! The plan was to prove to myself how he's so not worth my anguish.

"Hi," he's saying kind of muffled into my shoulder

because he's already scooped me into this big hug. Always gave great hugs Brian, nice firm hug-pressure.

"Hi," I say and my voice sounds so small in the din of the busy station, there are Raptors fans chanting some bullshit um, excuse me Toronto, in case you hadn't noticed two people are trying to have a moment.

We break apart and look at each other and I remember that we can't kiss and I feel weird because what the hell am I going to do with this insane glut of emotion that's cooked itself all up in me if I can't make it into kisses and give it away? I feel like my grandma when she cooks too much at Christmas and no one wants the leftovers. I straighten my shoulders and remind myself why I'm here. To be friends. To get closure.

"How are you?" he says.

"I'm good," I say. "How are you?"

"I'm all right. It's good to see you."

"You too, Brian."

"Um. You look great, Katy."

Yeah, no shit. The truth comes out: I took about two and a half hours selecting the perfect outfit for this occasion, I did indeed already pick it out in Montreal, I lied to Janet when I promised her over the phone that I wouldn't call him, all the while packing into my backpack my tights my black boots my denim skirt my cowboy shirt my mascara my perfume my tweezers my microwavable hair-removal wax my matching underpants and bra with the word "damn" stitched on them in rhinestones my lipstick my bronzer my hair putty my exfoliant my eye gel my pore tightener my oil control lotion. I'm feeling like a kind of unrealiable narrator right now, but believe me when I say it was for Tony's funeral that I came home. This was the tempting after-thought, a chocolate-covered hand grenade.

We start walking toward the CN Tower and I'm doing much better. We make cordial conversation about the Second Cup and what courses Brian's taking this fall. I diligently remind myself of Amber, Amber and I feel a little something for him, sure, but that's normal isn't it, isn't that to be expected? We walk along in the dark and I bump into him by mistake and giggle and he says, "We're like a robot vaudeville act."

"Always have been," I say and I'm laughing.

"Yeah. That's true."

And we're not in love, I get it, Amber Amber, but still I feel beautiful and well-lit and well made-up and Amber Amber Brian pays for us to go up. He pays! There's no line-up at this time of night and we just waltz right into the elevator and it just starts going up. It's always made me feel a little bit woozy and I've always reached out to grab Brian on our way up and tonight is no different and he doesn't even notice. Holding a scrap of his cute jean jacket we zoom up, up, kilometers into the air above the lights and noise of the city, to the top of the tower, a tower that once equaled the future and now is just a part of what is old and gray and around forever.

"It's really too bad you weren't here for the garbage strike in July, you know? Did you guys hear about that in Montreal?" he asks without even the tiniest catch in his voice to acknowledge that the big fat reason I wasn't here for the garbage strike is him him him. That pisses me off a little, but I don't call him on it. There's time for that later. I just want to be friends. The city below glints in the carafe of wine between us, our knees touch underneath our tiny table and I walk around in Brian's words, picking things up, scrutinizing them, taking in each detail. But being ever, ever so careful not to break a thing.

"Yeah, it was on the news. Did it stink?"

"It really did, you have no idea. At Spirits we had it all stacked up out back and it was just fucking rancid." Spirits. Where he works. With Amber. Amber. Right. "The whole city was just full of garbage. They did this collection at Christie Pits park, you know? And me and. Um. Amber dropped our garbage off there one day and it was just disgusting, like all leaking and shit. But the guys were really nice, the city guys. They put our stuff on a truck and drove it in and it just joined this huge mountain of garbage. In bags. It was even kind of nice in a way, like there were families and groups of roommates and stuff pulling garbage on little red wagons, you could see them coming from far away. All to Christie Pits. It was cool, like. I love when a huge city all of a sudden gets this community feel you know? It was really rad in a way, like kind of apocalyptic almost. And I kept thinking Garbage Strike. Shit. That's so a metaphor for *something*. Like, kind of metaphor. You know? That's kind of why I was thinking I wish you'd been here. It seemed like something you could've made something good out of."

It's true! Remember the time I compared love to a huge rolling ball of garbage? That was all right. It would have been *great* if I'd seen the garbage strike. So why did she get to see it? Amber! What kind of appreciation could a woman called Amber possibly have for something as foul and rotten and wonderful as a garbage strike?

"Um. What did Amber think of it?" I can't believe I've asked. It just slipped out. But I think my face is doing something resembling normal so maybe I can pull this off.

"Oh, you know, she just wanted it over I think. She's not really as into metaphors and stuff. I mean. Well, Spirits reeked and she works there more nights than me, so I guess she was just kind of sick of it from the beginning."

"Ah."

We look at each other. He pours more wine. He says, "It's really good to see you," and a little current has begun, a little current weaving underneath us, between our touching knees, I don't know what to think but this is going well this is going well this is going well Amber Amber, you know you sound irrelevant when he talks about you, you know he spends his days thinking of the sexy brilliance of my metaphors, my hot powers of observation.

"Oh!" Brian says, his face brightening. "I started doing some of the reading for the gender theory course I'm starting on Tuesday."

"Oh did you? How is it?" I can't believe school already starts on Tuesday. And I'm not going back. I would have taken that course, too.

"It's awesome. I mean, some of it makes no sense to me at all yet, and some of it is sort of really militant—"

"Nothing wrong with militant," I blurt.

"Oh sure, yeah, I guess I mean it just might take me a bit to get into. But some of the stuff makes what we learned in our theory class last year seem way more relevant. We have this French feminism anthology, that's what I started reading. These women are writing in the seventies and it's so revolutionary, but it just proves how slow stuff changes, you know? Like, right now your everyday liberal is happy to accept... or maybe ignore the fact that their society is built on all these phallocentric principles. And what that does. And these women were blowing up these myths so long ago."

"Yeah, people are really content to be like 'oh, feminism's arrived, it's solved everything, sexism doesn't exist any more.' I mean, women do it too."

"Oh, totally."

"And meanwhile we're sitting in the bar of the world's tallest free-standing penis."

Brian's face explodes into a grin. "No kidding! Like, this kind of architecture should totally be illegal! And no one even cares."

I love that he cares. And that he can laugh about it. "I know. Like, honestly. We can't be the first people to have noticed that our skyline is dominated by this huge erection." Some prissy-looking woman with perfect highlights at a nearby table is staring at me like I'm ruining her whole life and, needless to say, her date. I stare right back.

"Yeah, really. Like, they should have at least built the Skydome to look like a giant vagina. I mean, they kind of did I guess, but it could be so much better."

"Oh yeah. I mean, there should be like a clitoris-shaped observation deck."

"And it should glisten in the night."

"Gross."

"Yeah, yeah and once a month they set off red fire works."

"The Great Toronto Vulva. We really should build that. It's like that gay amusement park we were gonna make."

"The Back Door!"

"Yeah. You had to lube yourself up to get through the gates."

"Oh yeah, that was wicked." He is laughing. Hard. "God. I forget how to talk like this sometimes."

"I'm glad I'm here, too."

Suddenly Brian's face goes weird and he looks out the window at the sea of little lights. "Hey, listen," he says, looking back at me, but not at my eyes. "I wanted to apologize about being such an ass about that whole thing with the old guy."

"Oh. It's okay." I realize I've barely thought about Derek since my return to Toronto. I felt a rush of relief on the train ride here, knowing there was no chance of running into him for the next few days, and all my mental energy switched to the planning and staging of this very night.

"It isn't okay. I should have called you sooner. I'm sorry. I was just. You know, so fucked up about everything. I didn't really know if you wanted me to call or not, if it was, like, good for you or whatever. I mean, you were just gone. From one day to the next. I was so sad. I know that sounds like total bullshit knowing what you know now, but it's true. I missed you so much. I still miss you. It's just. Things are so fucked up."

"Yeah. They are."

"I'm sorry."

"It's okay."

When Brian is being serious, like now, a little Y-shaped vein in the top of his head bulges and his little eyes get really bright. We look at each other again. I mean we Look At Each Other. We don't say anything for a long, long couple of seconds but it's the good kind of not saying anything. It gets a little awkward but it's the totally wicked kind of getting a little awkward. And then our hands touch across the table because we both reached for the wine at the same time and I smile and bite my lip and try to suck in some air and throw a glance at all that Toronto all around us, and I look back at Brian and there are laughs in his eyes from the cheesy hand-touch and those great lips that I know are so soft are curling up at the edges. Oh, Amber. Amber. Drilling through me like a corkscrew twisting into a bottle, ripping me apart like pulling an orange in half, so juicy and ripe, this pain it's almost luscious you know, it seems like it's gonna be worth it, so worth it—

"You know it's really shitty that Tony died, but I'm so glad you're here."

"I missed you, Brian. A lot." I move my leg a little and hope he feels it. I'm not sure if he feels it. "So how are things with Amber anyway?" My voice is wobbly, but it needs to be asked.

"Mmmmokay." I knew it! "Mmmmokay" means bad. "Mmmmokay" means over. He smiles at me. When I don't smile back, the smile fades, he shakes his head.

"Why, Brian? I just don't understand why you did it."

"I don't know." Almost whispering this. "It doesn't make sense." He's leaning over the table, looking into my eyes, knees touching mine, looking so good, talking so quiet, just gorgeous, so right. "You're so great, Katy."

I lean across the table. I have my eyes closed. I can't wait to feel it again, it will be like that first time it will be like dancing it will be like—

Mmmmmmmmmmmmmmmmmmmmmmmmmmmmmmm
mmmmmmmmmmmmmmmmmmmmmmmmmmmmmmm
mmmmmmmmmmmmmmmmmmmmmmmmmmmmmmm
m m m m m m m m m m m m m m m m m m m m m m m m m m m
maaaaaaaaaaaaahhhhhhhhhhhhhhhhhhhhh

—this.

My whole body is soft, my whole life is complete, I never knew how badly I needed this until now. It would seem I've started talking although I feel like anything I might be doing now is the right thing to be doing. I feel like I'm in a champagne jacuzzi, sitting on a chocolate rainbow, dancing on a wheel of brie as big as the sun and I can be dumb or smart or talk or not and be happy happy happy for the rest of my life. I hear myself say, "I'll never, ever leave you again, Brian."

"Katy."

"I understand why you did what you did, it's okay. I forgive you. I mean, I did take off on you even before I knew, I think that we're even. Really. I don't mind. I just want to be with you. That's all I want. I forgive you for everything." Smiling so big and floating, floating. I take Brian's hand. It's small for a man's hand and I hold it in mine and I love it so much, every little hair on its back, each finger, remembering, relishing what each finger will do. To me. With me. Oh thank you. Thank God. Apparently now Brian is talking. I watch his sweet soft lips moving, his cute little adam's apple bounce up and down, try to pay attention, just want to kiss again, feel the table dig into my belly, so warm with wine, listen listen.

"Whoa, whoa, whoa," Brian is saying.

I'm suddenly cold, so freezing freezing cold. Why is he saying that? "Whoa" is a horse term. A term used to slow a slobbering, crazy horse.

Brian's Y-shaped vein is out and his eyebrows are sort of up and together.

"Katy," he says, "I'm sorry. I'm sorry. I shouldn't have done that. Shit. That. That wasn't the right thing to do. I'm. I am with Amber now. I want to be with her. I'm sorry. I'm sorry if I gave the wrong impression."

And I say,

"What?"

My brie rots, my rainbow melts and I fall hard on my ass. Brian wants to go, he thinks we should talk, he's sorry he's sorry he's sorry. He's holding my hand now and trying to bring me in close and he's whispering shit and the whole thing is not going well not going well I feel suddenly ill, suddenly very sober, suddenly very drunk, suddenly very heavy. I feel myself handing over money for the wine, I hear Brian and his polite-guy voice thanking the waiter, he has such a sissy polite-guy voice and I love it still, I love him still and this is probably the worst day of my life.

I stare at Brian like a confused kid and he stares back and all the laughs are gone from his eyes and he's looking at me like I'm being a bit embarrassing. But we kissed! We're in love! We're in love, godammit WE ARE IN LOVE. Shit. I can barely breathe, I want to burn this memory immediately but it is there for good, now, forever.

"I'm sorry Katy. I didn't know you felt that way still. I thought. I thought you wanted to be friends. I. I think we just got carried away."

"You didn't know I felt that way still." Just then, an anger telegram comes in: Motherfucker cheated on you stop motherfucker plays you like he wants you back stop motherfucker plays it like his new girl is nothing stop motherfucker KISSES you on top of the CN Tower stop motherfucker didn't know you *felt that way still* oh stop stop stop stop STOP!

"Fuck off!" I yell at Brian and push my chair away from the table with force and it goes kind of sideways and I pick up my purse and I kick the chair—I actually *kick* the chair—and I kind of stagger out of there and I've had half a litre of wine and my legs remind me and yeah! Yeah everybody stares at me on my way out and I don't give a flying fuck Okay? Okay? Is that OKAY? Jesus fuck oh Jesus here comes the snot again and the tears on my blushburnt skin, scalding the shit out of my face that everybody looks at as I leave, as I weave my way out into the tower. Brian behind me, "Katy! Katy!" not very loud, but I can hear him. He's coming after me, and I speed up and I want to throw up and I am so so so so so so embarrassed.

I mean, how did this even happen? Everything was fine. Everything was great. And then? And now. It's now. It's happened. I'm running away and I hear his voice and I just want to get away so I go down some stairs and I hope they go to where the elevator is I just want to get out of this tower, out of here God! If I just could have stayed where I was before the kiss I would've stayed there forever. I never would have known, it would have been a life of limbo but so much better than this. Shit. I can't find the elevator and Brian's finding me, I hear his voice I hear his steps and there's a part of me that's so glad he's following and man, that makes me sick. I push-stumble through a door and feel wind and relief and some of the tears get blown out of my face and I can see for a second. I'm standing on the outdoor observation deck of the tower, there's mesh fencing all around me and great big barriers keeping me from leaping out into the lights and I'm glad of that and my heart's just thumping. I see the city, my old city, and I see, for mere seconds it's true, but I see everything I have carefully convinced myself of over the past three months. I see the whole stack of contradictions that stood so precariously on each other's tiny polished surfaces. I see that I shined them up each day, in my head, each one of them like "he still loves me" and "it's just the wrong time" and "we're too young to have found each other but we'll be together when we're more mature" and "when I'm better in bed he'll take me back" and "Amber's just going to prove to him how much he really loves me". And the whole stack of them has just come down down down and it kills because I see now, right now in this moment just how hard, how fucking hard I worked on it. I painted and varnished and sanded and made perfect every little tiny delusion and they all just smashed on Horizon's Bar's tiled floor, shattered into sharp tiny shameful bits, blinking up at me, forsaken.

How? How did I let it get this far when I knew? I knew. I knew it was never ever going to last or be what I always wanted it to be. No. Not ever. Not when we lived together with the hanging plant, not when I held his heavy, sleeping body against me and just barely touched his face or his ear, holding my breath. I held my breath the whole time. And I left, for God's sake, I moved provinces so I could finally let it go. Nice try.

The late August wind can't dry my tears as fast as they're coming, I swear I don't even know where they come from any more and I'm also making "uh, uh, uh" noises, pretty loud ones, just as somebody puts their hands on my shoulders. Brian. I whip around and start hitting him, as hard as I can, hitting his stupid chest. I collapse against him, sobbing, slobbering, snotting.

"Fuck I hate you, Brian. Fuck! I hate you so much."

He folds his arms around me and I let him. I lean against him with all my weight, "uh, uh, uhhuhhuhuhhh."

"Hate me," he says. And that's a bit much frankly, that's a bit cheese and I push him away from me again, hard.

"Oh I fucking loathe you, Brian. Don't worry! I could fucking kill you." I think I could. If I could just heave him over these barriers, I think I'd do it and dive in after him. I have never been so humiliated in my whole entire life. Yeah. That's worth saying! "I have never been so humiliated in my whole entire life." And just when I'm sure I'd be ready, if I only carried a Swiss Army knife or a Leatherman or a lipstick or *anything* I would jam it in his eye and twist it till he *died*, the anger goes away again. It keeps doing that! Where does it go? I stand there and my shoulders turn in and I feel so small and it's so cold and windy and I take his hug again, I let him plant little kisses on top of my head. And they alternately comfort and revolt me because they make me feel like a little kid, his bratty kid sister who's just been beat up.

"You just ruined everything, Brian. You just ruined it all."

"It was ruined so long ago, Katy," he whispers.

"It was?" I don't think I've ever heard my voice this small before.

"It was. Katy. We haven't been right for so long."

This shuts me up for a second. I just stand there and shiver and shake.

"Do you want to go inside?" Brian asks.

"No!"

Brian leads me over to the concrete wall and we have a seat on the cold ground. I burrow my face into his lap, weeping, just letting it all out all over his pants, his wonderful corduroys.

"Remember," I say, between sniffles, "that time I phoned you at work? To tell you the dictionary definition of corduroys?"

"Yeah," he says, "It was 'trousers made of corduroy'."

"Yeah. That's so stupid," I say. We both laugh but only kind of and then I start crying again.

"I just," I sputter.

Brian is quiet. He has his fingers in my hair. He's moving them, kind of haywire.

"Was it really ruined so long ago?"

"I think it was. I'm sorry."

Slowly, slowly, between inhaling his thigh and feeling his fingers in my hair and wiping my nose again and again on his pants and "uh, uh, uh" ing all over the place a question comes floating into my head, just an innocent, cottony little question at first, but then I get suspicious of it and it laughs at me and it dares me so I go ahead and ask it, what more can go wrong?

"Was it gone even before Amber?" I ask. Another limbo moment, dammit, stop it here, I just want to stay here for a little while longer but no.

"I think so. Yeah. I think it was a long time ago."

"Oh God!" I wail. I don't know if I've ever wailed before. But this requires nothing less. This whole time I have reclined in the comfy talons of jealousy. I mean, at least it was somebody else standing in the way of my happiness. And now I know it's something far worse. He didn't love me. When I made him cards. He didn't love me. When I called him at work. He didn't love me. When I bit my lip and looked at him silly. He didn't love me. When I made him a special dinner. He didn't love me. Just now. When we laughed and talked and stared at each other and KISSED for Christ's sake. Oh God. Amber wasn't someone else. She was the only person. And I was gone. Already then.

"You didn't love me."

"I love you now."

"Fuck off." But something in me brightens. Because this is the first time he's said it. Ever.

"I should have said that before, Katy. I love you so much.

85

I'll always love you. But I wasn't *in* love any more. I'm sorry. I should have told you."

"Yeah, you fucking well should have." Such disgusting liquids and noises come out of me, things I didn't know my body had in it, things I'm kind of glad are coming out. All over Brian. And he sits and shakes. This goes on for a long time, I can't say how long, and he's making my hair so big, his fingers can't seem to stop.

Finally, when I've kind of resigned myself to staying here forever, to be found by tourists in the morning, a gnarled homage to the carnage of love frozen to the observation deck, Brian breaks the silence to say that he has to go inside somewhere, he's going to freeze to death and I follow him in, round the bend to the elevators where the operator stares at us and Brian says hi in his sissy polite-guy voice, trying to pretend like everything's fine. I'm surprised he doesn't tell the guy I have pink eye, but I'm sobbing and snorting pretty loud and there's no explaining that away so he just stands there and I hold his jacket again, all the way down looking out the big glass window as we plummet watching everything that was so tiny and fake-looking mere seconds ago become bulky and hard and life-size again.

"Seriously though Brian. What if I'd been better at the sex part?" I ask at the bottom of the tower and look up at him, still hopeful. This is insane. We're outside again, buildings looking down at us, cars screaming, sky pulsing with the weak weekly weekend promise of fun and fulfillment. We walk toward the station.

"I could be better Brian. Really!"

"Katy."

"I mean it. Answer me."

"Come on. Do you want to come over for awhile?"

"No. No, I'm going home. I have to go home."

"You can't drive now, Katy."

"Fuck you. Yes I can."

"I can't let you drive home right now. You're drunk, you're upset, you wouldn't even see the road. Just come over for a bit. Please. I want you to."

"Look, I don't exactly want to meet Amber."

"She's at her parent's place for the weekend."

"Fine!"

We get home. We go in. I look in at the hanging plant. Not even dead! Brian goes pee and I go to our old bedroom. There's his bulletin board, up beside his desk. There's the photo of me wearing a wig and drinking a Coke, half-covered by a YMCA schedule and there's a polaroid of him and Amber, together. They took it themselves in this very room. Smiling so big, so wide. Something is written at the bottom, something that I don't understand, not because it's not English but because it's a joke. Between them. She's cute, I'll admit it. But I dare say not much cuter than me. Same boob-size, same butt-size, my hair is a little bit puffier, but come on. What has she got? Brian's in the bathroom and he comes back in and sees me just staring at it.

"I'm sorry Katy."

"I know."

"Do you want anything?"

"No."

"Tea?"

"No!"

"Okay. I'm gonna make tea for me okay?"

"Fine. Of course. Why don't you just do everything in your whole life for you, Brian?"

"Katy."

"No, I mean it." I turn to him. He's leaning in the doorway like he's waiting for a bus. "You know, sometimes you are just the most selfish piece of shit I've ever met." My voice trembles, but the tears stay in.

"I'm sorry. I don't know what else to say. I didn't know what I was doing."

"Yeah, oh right, you had no idea what you were doing when you were fucking Amber? Maybe she's even worse than me!"

"Katy! Fuck. That is something you make up in your head! You were never bad at sex."

"But I wasn't good either. Was I?"

Brian is rubbing his face with his hands, the bedroom feels cold.

"Yes. Yes you were good. I don't know what you want me to say."

"I don't know either."

"I didn't cheat on you because of sex."

"Okay." Okay. Does that make me feel worse or better? My God, I can't tell. I sit down on the floor and look up at Brian. "Then what did I do wrong?"

"Nothing!" he snaps, but when I flinch his voice softens. "You didn't do anything. I'm sorry." The rug-hooked owl that Brian's grandmother made stares at us from the wall with mournful eyes. I guess I never *will* see Brian's grandmother again. I hope she tells him he's made a big mistake. "I'm going to make tea. Are you sure you don't want any?"

"Fine, I'll have some fucking tea." I grip my former carpet's little, shiny fibres with my sweaty hands, my nails dig into my palms, I don't want to be in this body now. I don't want to be awake.

Brian comes back with the tea and I tell him he's everything to me.

Brian looks at his feet.

I tell him I'll never meet another man who I love like I love him. I tell him that I thought of him the whole night that I was with Derek, that I thought Derek would help get rid of him. I tell him that it didn't work, that it just made things worse because after that night he was the only one I wanted to call, the only one who understands me. I tell him that the way we talk to each other is like talking to no one else, it takes no effort at all, it just happens and how can he throw that away? I tell him he'll never, never find that again. I tell him he's beautiful and I tell him that I love how he kisses and how he smells and that I picture our wedding every single day at least once, at least quickly before I blink it away and I tell him a hundred more things that a sobbing, pitiable thing has said a hundred times in every kind of art and every kind of life that's ever been made.

Brian looks alternately at his feet and at the rug-hooked owl.

Do you know what these arguments are like? The kind where the end happened already? They're boring and they're long. I make my case, again and again, for why our relationship should have been the most important, basically only worthwhile thing in Brian's life and he repeatedly tells me that he's sorry but that it's not the same for him. He tells me he doesn't know what to say. I cry some more. We drink some tea. I make snarky comments, Brian takes them, I'm convinced he's just humouring me. I yell at him for that. He says I'm the most beautiful person he's ever known, he brushes my hair out of my tear-sticky face, I want him to kiss me so so bad and tell me this is all just a joke, just a test of my devotion to him, that he's crazy for me, that Amber never existed, that he'll never let me go. Surprise! He doesn't. Brian lies down on the floor, yawning. This makes me mad because I'm still pumped. I think another go round is probably the one that'll break him, if I just tell him one more time how much I love him, how I will never meet another man who gets me like he does, if he just hears it one more time he'll finally cave. But he's falling asleep. He used to do this all the time. I'd still be talking, I'd still want to snuggle a little more and he'd be gone. He'd still talk to me, but it wouldn't make any sense, it was just interactive dreaming. Once he told me about the hippos he was growing when I told him he was the best thing that had ever happened to me. He doesn't mean to do it, he just can't stay awake.

"Do you mind if we get in bed?" Brian asks through a yawn. "I'm cold."

"I'm not sleeping here. I'm going home. I just wanted to say everything now because I can never speak to you again." I say this regally. It's the first thing I'm proud of saying for the past four hours.

"You can't go home. It's four AM."

"I'll take a cab."

"To your car?"

"Yeah."

"I really don't think you should drive tonight. You're too tired."

He's right. I can barely see.

"I can't sleep with you."

"I'll sleep on the floor."

"Okay."

It's freezing in the house and I pack myself into our old bed, my every skin cell slightly panicked at the idea of bits of Amber touching me. Brian lies down on the floor beside the bed, wrapped in the smallest of the two blankets. He pulls his knees right up to his chest.

"Goodnight, Katy," he says from down there and I look at him and he looks so sweet and pathetic. I start to laugh, a bitter and annoyed little laugh. This man has scooped out my insides and put them on the barbecue, smacking his lips and shaking on salt. I have never loved anyone so much.

"Get into the bed for fuck's sake. How could this night get any worse?"

"Are you sure?"

"Yes."

He climbs in. How many times have I thought to myself, "I would give anything for just one last night, to sleep beside him one last time." I wriggle as close to the wall as possible and start crying again. The wall has a sort of faux brick finish that used to freak me out, but now I kind of feel it would be useful to scratch my face against. On second thought I'm too tired. I feel something poking into my back. I turn around. It's Brian, poking the corner of a Kleenex box into me.

"Here," he says. Worseorbetter?

I grab it, roll over and hear him begin to breathe hard and heavy. He's asleep. I lie there for a couple of minutes, maybe seven, sniffling away when suddenly another question sails in, this one not soft at all, but hard and knocking, so I wake him up. I have never done this in all the time I've known him and it actually makes me feel stronger to pull him out of sleep.

"Did you ever love me, Brian? I mean were you really in love with me?"

"Mmmhmm. Yeah."

Gone again. Fuck. Did he mean it? Does it matter?

As I drift off to sleep, I fart in the bed. Twice. I can't even help myself but it's not like I try. This makes me smile, ever so slightly, through all the stuff coming out of my face as I finally, finally give in.

I wake up to a soft grumble of thunder and rain spattering the window. I'm still in that moment, you know the one, that tiny little moment every morning where everything is absolutely wonderful and you're all warm and cozy and your sleep-heavy brain isn't working yet until BLAM the gears start turning, chunk chunk, memory squeaks into play and. I. Remember. I look over. Yup. Still there. Brian, mouth open, nose whistling, beautiful. I jump out of bed like I'd like to jump out of myself. The ridiculous, horrible things I said last night are pelting my conscience, it's time to gather up what dignity I can and go. I go to the bathroom, I pocket some tiny bottle of bullshit expensive perfume that's clearly Amber's. I come back into the bedroom, squared shoulders, hard face, ready to leave for good and all and Brian is sitting up in bed, blinking his little eyes. How can I still think he's the cutest? But he is! Oh dammit if you could only see him. He is just the cutest. I keep my mouth in a line I hope.

"I'm going," I say.

"I get it now," he says, blinking. "I didn't get it last night. But I get it now. You're never going to speak to me again."

"You got that right," I say.

"I can't... I can't take that."

"You have no choice, Brian."

"I'm so sorry, Katy. I love you."

I can't help it, that grabs me by the tummy and gives a little twist. "God, Brian. I really wish you would have told me that at a better time."

"So do I. I really. I wish it wasn't so goddamn hard for me to say. I wish I could say it before I fuck something up completely." And he starts crying! Oh my God. As if I need this! I accidentally divide completely in two with a big noisy rip. One half stands there and taps her foot and sucks her teeth and acts how I meant to act this morning, generally disgusted and ready to go, while the other half, and here's the really repugnant part, goes over to him and says, "Awww, Brian," and gives him a hug and a kiss on the cheek and says she's sorry. Sorry! Hello? Is there another one of those angergrams coming in? I could seriously use one.

Unfortunately the simpy moron me is the one that Brian sees and he hugs back and says over and over how sorry *he* is and oh man oh man oh man.

"I feel like I ruined your whole summer," Brian says,

wiping his eyes.

"Don't flatter yourself!" pops out of me and it shocks me how bad our dialogue has become. It's almost enjoyable at this point, let's face it, it's been enjoyable since Brian started crying.

"I didn't mean it like that. I just don't know what I'll do without you. I never even imagined that I couldn't talk to you."

I wish I'd said, "You can talk to Amber," and walked out the door, but instead I say, "Oh man. This fucking sucks." Brilliant.

"Stay for breakfast?"

"I have to go."

"Please."

Brian has never ever begged me for anything. And I have to say that I really like it. Unhealthy as it may be, I agree to stay and he dashes off to the kitchen. He proudly emerges with a stainless steel pot full of Special K, milk and two spoons. I almost start to cry, but try to eat some cereal to stave it off.

"I can't eat this," I say and let the spoon fall. Brian takes the pot and starts to eat. I start crying again, but this time just a little bit, real nice and pathetic. Brian puts the pot on the ground and holds my hand. We sit and watch the Special K putrefy in the milk.

"I'd rather have a prostate operation every day than never talk to you again."

"What?" I say.

"I mean it."

"No you don't, Brian."

We look at the cereal some more and think about it.

Finally he walks me to the front door and we hug. For maybe an hour. We both cry some more. I get snot all over the shoulder of his sweater. He promises he'll never wash the sweater again. We shake from lack of sleep and agony.

"I hope you're happy with Amber," I say. "Treat her nice." I do mean it, I think.

"I'll miss you so much," says Brian.

I say, "Just pretend I'm teaching in Japan for a really long time. And can't call you. Or email you."

"But the Japanese are so technologically savvy!"

We end on a grin. Forever. We end for forever on a really stupid joke. A kiss on the cheek. The door whooshing shut. Me out in the rain wearing dirty clothes and a puffy face. Brian waving out the window, me stomping through mud puddles until College station sucks me down into Toronto's slippery, steamy, rot-smelly belly.

When I get home, there's a police car in the driveway. Terrific! I go in and there's my mother at the table, bawling, my father with his arm around her saying "bleached blonde hair" to a short, bored-looking police woman. Missing! I've gone missing! Genius. I can't believe I didn't even phone.

"I'm here," I call. My parents come running over to me, they hug me and kiss me and my mom cries all over the place.

"Oh thank God, Oh thank God!" they say over and over again.

The police woman packs up, mutters goodbyes and slips

past us, out the door, into her car, down the driveway and my mother's arms are still around me. My father is pacing back and forth and apparently scrutinizing our hallway ceiling lamp.

"I'm so sorry," is all I can think of to say, and my mother asks me again and again why I didn't phone and I tell her no reason no reason no reason and I feel so hollowed out, just rotted through and not even crying any more. Not even crying because my mom is crying, not even crying because my dad's not talking, not even crying when I realize that the MuchMusic of my mind is currently showing a soft-core porn of Brian and I in the shower cuddling till the water gets cold and I don't notice and Brian turns the water off and steps out of the tub. I say I'm sorry again and I shake my head and disengage myself from my mother. It's embarrassing to me that she's this upset and I can't even get the tears to start. My father hugs me then, pretty hard and breaks away fast and says, "Jesus, Katy, we thought you were dead," while he fluffs up my hair and tries to give his everything's cool smile and then he can't do it and he looks away on the word dead and then stares up at the ceiling light again, the 60 watts glittering in his eyes. Brian and I are having a post-shower snuggle in my head and I hate myself so much at this moment, I just want to focus on now and how I've done a bad thing and how much these people love me and how much better that actually is in the long run. I want to focus on the nice smell of my house that reminds me of being a four year old running around in pajamas with feet. I want to focus on the fact that I've always been surrounded by suburban comfort and warmth and love and Christmas and education and laughs and fights that had making up at the end and pictures on the walls of me at all ages, and I've never been cold and I've never been hungry for longer than twenty minutes so why am I not the happiest creature in the world? How can I feel this bad?

"I'm gonna go make some lunch," says my dad and heads into the kitchen and my mom gives a kind of embarrassing kind of beautiful teary smile. But then it goes away. Her face darkens. She looks me in the eye. We stand in our front hall, shifting our weight from one foot to the other, making the hardwood floor creak.

"Do you have any idea," my mom says, "how worried we were?"

"I'm really, really sorry," I say. "I'm going upstairs. I need to be alone." I start to go, but my mom's in my way, arms folded across her chest.

"Where the hell did you go, Kate?"

"I went out with Brian, okay?" The tired way she's looking at me makes me feel like shit. "Look, I just had the worst night of my life, it's about all I can handle for this weekend, I really just want to go have a nap."

My mother's eyes flash. It is rare that we fight in earnest but when something ignites, the flames spread fast.

"Oh, *you* had the worst night of your life, did you? Did you by any chance also spend the night petrified that your only daughter had died in a fiery car crash?"

"What, do you think I did this on purpose, do you think I set out to scare you, Mom? I forgot to call you, it's true, but I was too busy watching my life falling apart, okay? So sorry. Maybe you could spare me the melodrama." I try to make a getaway into the kitchen, but my mom follows me, shrieking at my back. My tall, quiet dad is making tuna salad and doesn't even look up when my mom stomps in. She's shorter than me and is wearing a purple sweatsuit, but she's still intimidating the hell out of me. I stare out the kitchen window at our deck, our sunburnt back yard.

"Spare *you* the melodrama?" my mother screams. This woman lives to speak in italics. "You have got to be joking, Miss Katy, Princess Melodrama herself. I'm not the one carrying on about a man who *cheated* on me as if he's God's gift to women! Honestly, the way you've blown this Brian relationship out of proportion is getting ridiculous. Is he still with that other girl?"

I whirl around. "Yeah. He is."

"Then why the hell were you going out with him in the first place? You're not acting rationally."

"Rationally? We lived together, Mom! We shared a life. Does that mean nothing to you? How am I supposed to act rationally?"

"Lived together! Out of *his* financial necessity. You were perfectly happy living with the girls in first semester as I remember it, but oh no, you upended it all because *he* couldn't afford to pay his rent, because he would move in with you as long as you did all the work and found a cheap apartment." My father bangs around in the fridge.

"What are you saying? I tricked him into it?"

"No, I'm saying he couldn't have cared less, one way or the other. That was always Brian's way, just do whatever is convenient for him."

"You don't know what you're talking about, Mother. He

loved me."

"Oh, and that's why you would call me in tears at least once a month asking if it was normal that he hadn't said it yet?"

"He said it yesterday!"

"Listen to yourself, Katy! Yesterday? You're not together any more. Grow up."

"Jesus, Mom, do you really have to rub it in my face today of all days?" I try my best to look downtrodden even though I'm feeling ready to fight.

"Yes! Actually, today of all days is *exactly* the time to do so my dear because today I've had no sleep because I thought you were dead and all you can do is simper and whine and defend Brian. I'm sick of it, Kate. You're a smart girl. Move on. You're not the first human being to fall in love. You need to get some perspective."

"That's what you always fucking say."

"That's because I'm always fucking right." The F-words are out, we clearly mean business. "I thought you'd finally get it once you moved away, I hoped you'd finally meet someone new and realize that what you had with Brian is a far cry from love."

"How can you pretend to know what we felt for each other, Mom? Of course I try to meet other guys. I do. And there's no one. I've been there two and a half months and I haven't seen *anyone* who would be remotely good. I see tons of cute guys, dreamy little French boys, they come into my work in droves. But then I think about it and it makes me want to puke. Because like, it just doesn't make sense to be in love with anybody else because Brian is the one I love. You know? Like he's the truth. And anyone else is just… just like a stand-in. It's… it's like in soap operas, it would be like 'the role of Brian will now be played by whoever' and then you think man, I really liked the old Brian way better, you know? Like, he had better hair and he just delivered the dialogue way better. Because it's not ever going to be the same again. It'll be staged. I can't. I can't make myself look pretty the way I did for him for some *other* dude, that's just ridiculous. It's just like doing a shitty, shitty community theatre version of the Broadway smash. I mean, seriously Mom, how can I have perspective on something that just means everything and can never and will never mean anything less?" I've delivered this entire polemic at full volume, gesticulated wildly and now I'm breathing heavy, staring at the kitchen floor. My father takes the opportunity to slink away with three tuna sandwiches stacked on a plate.

"And you say *I'm* melodramatic," my mother says quietly, with control. She can be such a bitch and I wish I could be more like her and I wish I was nothing like her at all.

"I wish I'd never moved, Mom. I wish I'd never let you talk me into it." Someone to blame! How gratifying, how freeing. It's somebody's fault—my mother's—the perfect scapegoat for any dire situation. My mother did this to me.

"Maybe if you lived life outside of your own stubborn head for just a minute, you'd remember that Brian cheated on you before you left him."

"But if we'd at least been in the same province we could have worked it out."

"No, Katy. You're wrong. You just aren't right for each other. And there are so many opportunities in Montreal.

That's the main reason I thought you should go. There are such great schools there Katy, they have creative writing at Concordia, you're so good at that—"

"Whatever, Mom, the only reason you wanted me to move was so you could live through me. You totally suckered me into going because you're bitter that you never could be the coked-out disco slut you always wanted to be."

"Pardon?" Icy.

"I mean come on, that's what you always wanted right? You wish you'd bought those silver stiletto boots, wish you'd slept around a bit before you settled down, before you'd had me."

"How dare you say—"

"Let me tell you something Mom. Being a slut isn't all it's cracked up to be. At least I learned that much in Montreal, so thanks a lot for making me go." I realize what I've said and I feel sickness grab my throat, my face goes limp. I lean against the counter and look out the window some more.

"For the love of Christ, Katy, I never wanted to be a slut. I certainly never wanted you to be one! What the hell are you trying to tell me? What have you been doing?" My mom's eyes are ripped open, wide.

"Nothing," I say to the window, completely defeated and I think maybe I should tell her about Derek, but would it just scare her more? Would she just be ashamed? Would she think I was as stupid as I know I am?

"Are you sleeping around Katy? Is that your rebellion?"

"No!" God, if she knew the truth! And I'm mad again, rip-roaring.

"That's normal, I think, a normal reaction to heartbreak. I just want you to make sure you're being safe and—"

"Mother!" I run out of the kitchen, bound up the stairs, two at a time. "You. Don't. Fucking. Know. Me. At. All." One word per bound, and then I'm in my room, I slam the door behind me and hear my mom's voice, muffled and sad from the bottom of the stairs.

"Katy! Please. Don't shut me out." After about a minute, I hear the floor creak as she walks away.

Sitting on my single bed, I look at the ducks that waddle around the tops of my walls, the border I picked when I was seven. I grab a stuffed pig from my bed and whip it at the wall, hard. I grab a fuzzy elephant and do the same. Teddy bears a lion a parrot a fuzzy frog, I nail them all against the wall, against my bookshelves, whirling crazy around my little girl room. Then I sit on my bed and stare at the carnage until the window goes dark.

It must be ten o'clock by the time I tiptoe downstairs, hoping my parents are in bed. I need to eat. I bring my wodge of leftover quiche and two peaches into the family room, psyched to watch rifts form and heal in twenty-two minute intervals. My chest squeezes when I notice first the absence of Tony's kiddy pool, then my father sitting in the corner chair, reading a golf magazine.

"Hey Dad," I say and sit down on the couch.

"Hi," he says. He looks so sad and worn out. I swear his beard is greyer than when I last saw him. He watches me eat for a minute, then says, "Your mother was under a lot of stress this afternoon. I mean, considering Tony's just died and everything, it was a lot to take."

"I know," I say. "But she was still being really harsh."

"You know, this time I don't think she was." My dad fiddles with the collar of his golf shirt. "She knows what she's talking about. It's time to move on."

"God Dad, you always take her side," I mumble, my mouth full of quiche. "I just want to be left alone."

"I only take her side when she's right, Kate. This Brian character's no good for you. We're worried about you."

"Well, you don't have to worry because I'm never talking to him again."

"Well, good. Because he's making you very selfish. And I know you're not that way, Katy."

I can barely get the quiche past the lump in my throat. "Yeah. If you don't mind, I just want to eat in peace."

He breathes in loudly and exhales into his magazine and I turn on the TV and chew hard with guilt slowly, steadily inflaming my brain.

On Monday, Labour Day, I leave my family with awkward, terse goodbyes and I get on a train and read some *Cosmo* and zip past streaks of lake and beach and rock and river that fill the five hours between the two cities that aren't quite my home. Some barely suppressed, frenzied laughter at *Cosmo*'s advice to "mash up a little papaya and put it into the entrance of your vagina" and some coffee and some Pepsi and an overpriced turkey sandwich with no mayonnaise or mustard or *anything* on it and the sleep-sour taste of the sandwich an hour and a nap later I am ready for Montreal. I guess I'd better be, I've burned every bridge I had to Toronto within a three day visit. But I'll show my mom a thing or two. This time I'm ready for real. To live alone, to be single. I will buy myself candles. I will spend great evenings reading the books I've promised myself for years to read. I'll really *think* about what it means to be a woman and I'll unroll the old mat and start doing yoga again. Then I'll feel bourgeois so maybe I'll volunteer at a soup kitchen and get involved in prostitute advocacy. I'll learn to make pickles! This is what I've always needed, yes, this is what I want and I've forgiven him, I've decided. I've moved on. It's time to take a lover, to see the world. No! To be happy in my own skin, in my own space! Dammit. Dammit. I mean what is this little post-breakup breakdown in the grand scheme of things? I mean seriously. There are wars, there's famine and then there's my busted up heart? Get real. You didn't really think I was gonna dwell on this forever did you? You didn't honestly think I couldn't have perspective on the situation? See Mom? I'm doing just fine. I'm gonna improve my French! It's beautiful. I'm beautiful. Brian's beautiful. He didn't mean to hurt me. I didn't mean to get hurt. It's all just one huge, mad coincidence and I stumble out into Montreal bug-eyed and pushy on the platform, just raring to go and completely terrified of stopping, even for a moment.

I dump my stuff and say hello again to my tiny apartment and truly appreciate for the first time its sloping fake wood flooring and closet-sized kitchen complete with three rotting bananas and armies of fruit flies and I finally, finally take down my photo of Brian with the hanging plant and put it under my bed to get dusty with Brian's soft blue t-shirt that's already under there, and I let out a yelpy sigh of success. Then I bolt through the door again, scramble out into the night. The air blowing up my skirt is cooler than any air I've felt in this province before and it must be a sign, it must be a symbol and it all feels so right and I can't wait to tell Janet that I'm done and I'm ready and I'll tell her about Tony and my parents because really that's all more important than stupid crappy Brian Johnson anyway and I whump my way through the Second Cup door. Orange streetlamps from across the street refract in the chrome of the espresso machine and give the place this kind of sexy post-summer glow. The tall front windows are open, letting in that slightly stiff September breeze that's screaming freedom at the top of its fine Fall lungs, harmonizing with happy people sipping, slurping, chatting this perfect Labour Day away.

"Janet!" I practically sing. She's bussing tables, clutching the gray plastic bussing-bin, laughing and beautiful, leaning against the long, high table where I first met Derek, laughing and now throwing her head back and I watch her for a second because she hasn't heard me. Then my eyes drift to the customer who's made her laugh so hard, thinking maybe it's her friend Lee who I really can't help but like, and I'm smiling big and hard, words all formed in my gullet, at the ready like machine gun rounds.

No. My entire body goes gummy, fear zips up and down my spine like spiders on speed. Derek. Derek and Janet. Talking. Laughing. My face feels hot, my ears are burning, I don't think I'm even blinking, just staring at his jowly, slimey smile, that's him all right and now Janet's seen me, and as my symbolic systems so often do, the light and the wind take a dramatic turn for the worse. The sexy post-summer glow sparks and flares into something resembling a cartoon of hellfire, flames licking Janet's stunned face and the wind gives up its lame warmish breeze act, comes right out and says it: it's cold. I have the goosebumps to prove it.

"Hey!" says Janet, totally trying to squeeze out of her caught-face and into a smile, pretending there's nothing to be caught at at all, pretending we always serve each others' molesters vanilla lattés while the other one goes home for a *funeral*.

"Yeah hey," I say like a bitch and I turn around to go and a sucker-punch of dread nails me in the belly when I realize there's not a single place I can go where I won't feel alone. But I have to get out of there, seeing him again makes my skin crawl, makes me remember too much. I hear Derek say, "Oh Jesus" as I walk out and the icy wind of the September night reaches up my skirt and pinches my ass and tries to spank me until I yell, "Fuck" loudly enough to stop it. Janet has come out to the sidewalk to stand with her arms crossed over her golf shirt and to stare at the gum pounded into the pavement.

"I didn't know you'd come in tonight," she says, quietly, not looking up.

"Tonight? You mean there have been other nights? I've only been gone for three days!" I feel like my insides, already grated raw by the weekend's festivities just can't take another twist or even tickle.

"No no. We only hung out one other night," Janet says, shrugging her shoulders as if she's telling someone, "I've never actually been much into chocolate."

"Hung *out*?" I say, "As in outside of the café?"

"Just last night," Janet says and looks at the ground

again. She takes a deep breath. "I slept with him."

She might as well say she also slept with Brian and murdered Tony, I don't stick around to hear any more, I tear down Ste. Catherine, head down, gripping the bottom of my skirt, gnawing on my bottom lip, cursing and swearing. Some guy yells, "Hey, baby!" from across the street and I don't look up, I just give him the finger and I don't put it down the whole way home. Anger is all I've got to fight the sick that seeing Derek has shot through me so I slam my way back into my apartment and just hate her and just hate him and just hate hate hate Brian too, yup he's back, from beyond the "I'm over it" grave Brian careens into my rage and fuck fuck fuck fuck fuck them, I start to do the only thing at this point I know how to do which is follow my body into the kitchen and try to pay attention because when I'm mad my body tends to do some crazy things and this time round I grab the rotting bananas from their frothy wreath of flies and start peeling their pungent brown skins and I whip the skins—fuck them—at the wall and I throw the bananas—fuck them—in a bowl. They're so old and soft that they break into halves and thirds and stringy bits hang off the severed ends. Wielding a fork, I glare into the bowl, pleased with the bananas' pallor and bruisy bits. And no, the symbolic potential here has most certainly not eluded me— I am perfectly aware that the banana is the head-honcho of the phallic fruits as I slam my fork down into the middle and watch the well-formed flesh press paste-like through the fork's cold tines. "I'll give you phallocentric, Brian," I mutter under my breath. I have decided to bake muffins. "Metaphor Muffins!" I scream like Betty Crocker gone bad.

In fact, as I mash and skewer the fruit I am swearing like the apocryphal sailor, including such stellar constructions as "fucking fuck motherfucker" and "asshole piece-of-shit prickhead" in my diatribe. There is mashed banana joining its former skin on the wall, my fork dings the metal bowl with each blow, with each loud, increasingly raspy curse of everything that has ever once, even by mistake, aided in making me feel this way. So that would be Brian. And Derek. And Janet. And the very fact that Janet is on this list. And my mom. And my dad. And myself for treating them like shit.

"Oh fuuuuuuuuuuuck!" I scream, letting my high, screechy register in on the fun for a moment.

"Shut the fucking fuck up!" thunders a baritone voice from. From where? Is it God? Oh shit! Is it God?

"People are fucking trying to sleep!" the voice says again and I realize, prodding my banana carrion with renewed vehemence, that it's just my goddamn neighbour, maybe you remember him? The old man who lives across the fire escape from me who screams at the world daily at six AM because he can't find his comb or his cat knocked his water over.

"Yeah fuck you!" I yell as I yank open my kitchen curtain, "I'm just getting you back for all the times you woke me up."

"Fuck you I said quit your fucking talking you lazy slutty bitch!" I'd normally actually be nervous if someone yelled that at me, but since my blood's already reached a rolling, foaming boil, I can only credit the guy for being that hardcore. I see his crazy face, framed with erratic tufts of hair like gray grass poking through patio stones. He's wearing the type of tank-top classically referred to as a Wife Beater and he's blinking wildly and wrinkling up his nose.

"Don't you fucking call me a slut, you ugly lunatic!" I yell, at which point I hear the window of the guy who lives below me slide open. He's a nineteen year old named Jimmy from Vancouver who invariably struts around with no shirt on, his nipples jutting out like ju-jubes iced on a ginger bread house. I duck back behind my curtain into the safety of my kitchen. I crack an egg into the banana bowl and listen to Jimmy ream out the old man for waking him up, hear him threaten that he's going to call the landlord again if the yelling doesn't stop this week, at which the old man bellows further profanity through his smudged window into the garbage filled gulf between our two buildings. The old man keeps it up long after Jimmy has stopped and I put an eye to the crack between my curtain and the window, watching him blink as if his life depended on it and wrenching his nose up and down like a caffeinated rabbit.

When I wake up the next day at one PM after cursing and baking and sobbing myself to sleep, I have a wicked rage hangover complete with embarrassment, gutrot and a rubbery, function-free feeling in my brain. I hazard a glance into my kitchenette and see that it was no dream: I for real and true massacred bananas, baked them into muffins, washed the bowls, put them away, like a fifties mom with benzedrine withdrawal. The muffins sit, looking awfully well-formed and golden, on a plate in a proud pyramid, chopped imagery whipped into tidy consumable products. I have gotten out of bed now, I am staring at my handiwork, wide-eyed, worried.

Am I going crazy? Am I losing my proverbial shit? I yelled louder last night than the guy who gets eviction threats, the latest of these thanks to my ranting. I'm such a jerkface. And a coward. No wonder my friends stab me in the back, no wonder my lovers cheat on me. It sounds maudlin, I know, but really, I think I'm maybe starting to get it. I'm self-absorbed. I'm obsessive. I'm loud. I shellac what I really feel with noisy, sticky, obvious jokes so haphazardly, so willy-nilly that when my emotions finally do bust loose they shatter that sloppy, hardened shell with such force that wit-shrapnel whacks passersby in the face—wit-shrapnel? God! Shut up! And that! *This* is the worst part. Not only is all of the above true, I also can't stop spewing it all out, I can't stop making it into sentences, packing it into paragraphs, wrapping it in parts and giving it out as if all of my garbage is worthwhile as long as I shake on the right similes, squeak in a little narrative drive. And now there's more plot than I know what to with; I didn't even want one in the first place!

I grab a muffin and eat it. Within seconds. I grab another and eat it, too. Somewhere in the corners of my head I hear the twangy bass of "Seinfeld" and I think I must truly be asylum-bound when I realize that it's my neighbour watching TV. I can always sort of hear it, the walls and windows are paper-thin, I can hear coughs and nose-blows, I've adapted to it. But seemingly my brain is so sick of it's own whinging and hurting that it's letting outside noise in to drown itself out. I open my kitchen curtain, munching my muffin and watch the old man watch his crummy TV. He's wearing pajama pants with his undershirt today, rather than the usual briefs. I guess this is his Fall look. He doesn't look angry, in fact pretty placid. There are beer bottles all over the table, but other than that the place looks clean enough. His slightly skinny cat sits on the arm of his chair and watches "Seinfeld" with him and he absently pets her head except for every thirty seconds or so when he ferociously scratches one of his weedy tufts of hair and the scalp underneath. The sweetness of my muffin starts to gross me out as I remember Jimmy threatening to rid the building of him. For what? For calling me a lazy slutty bitch? Not even. Just because he said it too loudly.

"Katy. God. I really have to explain this whole thing to you." It's Tuesday and Janet has accosted me at Dagwood's sub shop where she knows I take my lunch break when I work a day shift.

"Yeah," I say, as coldly as I can, "maybe not while I'm choosing sub toppings." I can't even believe I'm talking to her at all, let alone quipping. I mean *Derek*. Jesus. But I don't feel like leaving, and she keeps looking at her feet, even when she orders her mortadella and extra olives and she happily happily pays for my sandwich, saying, "It's on me" with the kind of gusto that proves just how horrible she is feeling at this moment and that if she could have one wish it would be that this would be enough: that buying me a sandwich would sew up this gash in my heart and my trust and she would be my best girl again. Or am I wrong? Maybe she can't wait to get back to her apartment where Derek is waiting, curled and wrinkly in her bed, sipping jasmine tea. I shiver.

We sit down across from each other and I look straight

at her, leaned over my Pepsi, sipping through my straw.

"Stop looking at your feet for a second," I say.

She looks up at me, tentatively, flinchingly, like I'm going to spit in her face or poke her eyes out or something. This annoys me. A lot. She should be ready to accept either of those eventualities. Looking at her longer makes me feel sort of bad. We've never really fought before. I think the closest we ever came was this time when Janet dissed my *Cosmo*-reading habit and I defended it long-windedly—rather astutely I'll add now that I'm in this position of power.

"I'm sorry, Katy. I'm so sorry." Janet has carefully unwrapped her sandwich and now looks down at it and cries gently.

"It's just really ironic, isn't it?" I say icily, in the direction of the green vermiculite counter.

Janet pokes a finger into her soft, white sub bun and watches intently as the indent attempts to rectify itself. I watch, too.

"I guess it is," she says finally, "I know it wasn't right."

"The whole time, Janet. The whole time you were telling me how he assaulted me, that it wasn't my fault—"

"It wasn't!"

"You almost had me convinced. I was starting to feel better and now I feel even stupider than ever. I must be, like, the worst judge of character in the history of the world!" I snort and look away. It surprises me sometimes how loudly I can snort. Shit. The young women working the counter are staring but trying not to. They slice tomatoes with long, sharp knives and make stern tomato slicing faces but I'm on to them.

When I look back at Janet she has poked a few more violent holes into the top of her sub and a bit of dressing is oozing out of one them. Mine is still in its packaging, another fat dull phallus between myself and my only friend.

"Look, I have to explain this to you, it's not as simple as it sounds."

"Jesus, Janet. I mean, why the fuck would you ever even *talk* to that disgusting assbag?" After all these months anger has finally grabbed me by the collar and is shaking me hard.

"I. I talked to him because I wanted to tell him that what he did was disgusting."

"Great!" I snort. This is becoming a veritable snort party.

"It's true, I'm serious. Saturday night I went out drinking, at the Cock and Bull with Lee and this girl Frieda and a few other people and then I went into the Cup to check the schedule because me and Aaron switched our Sunday shifts but I wanted to make sure. So I go in there, and I'm all drunk right, and then he's sitting at the counter, all haggard looking and I think he was drunk too and he calls me over."

"Uh huh."

"And I go up to him and I go 'you are one sick fuck, you know that? You're not welcome here.'"

"You said that?"

"Swear to God. You can ask him."

"Yeah, I don't think I'll be talking to him any time soon."

We look at our subs for a minute.

"So what did he say?" I finally ask because I don't know what else to say to make her start talking again and I'm dying to know what he thought. She's just massacring her sandwich with her thumb nails, forming little guilt-runnels of Dagwood sauce all over the waxed paper.

"He said that you had every right to feel that way."

"He did?" This actually catches me off guard.

"Yeah. He said at first, when he found the returned necklace and everything he was really angry and insulted and stuff and he felt totally betrayed—"

"*He* felt betrayed!" I yell. This is too much.

"I know. At first I didn't buy it either, but then he told me that the reason he was at the Cup in the first place was to talk to you. He wanted to explain his side of the story to you, he said he had grown to understand what had happened and how it had been misperceived on both ends."

"Yeah, that sounds like Derek-speak all right."

"Well, I told him I really didn't think you'd want to see him. And then I'm right about to leave when I look out the window and Lee and Frieda are making out!"

"What an asshole!" I say, in spite of myself. The Dagwood's women have given up their tomato-slicing ruse by this point and are blatantly staring. I can't say I wouldn't do the same if I were them.

"Yeah," Janet continues, "they said they were staying out to smoke. And I was so drunk and I've just been feeling so shitty about Lee lately anyway, especially that night, and then he sees me watching through the window and you know what he does? He waves at me! And he has his same old charming smile on, just like he always does and he's playing with the ties on Frieda's coat at the same time and I just waved a go-away wave, I don't know why, I just didn't feel like having him around any more.

"So I just keep sitting there on the stool, sort of not even conscious of where I am, you know. And Derek asks me if I'm okay and I sort of snap out of it and I'm like 'listen, I think you're the last person to help me right now.' And he says again how he really wishes that he could explain things to you."

"What the hell was he gonna say if I *had* been there?" I ask.

"That's what I said! I was like, 'Derek. You fucking went down on her! What's to explain?' and he said he knows now that he had no right to do that, he just thought things were different for you. He said he thought you were more. Well, he said he thought you were more like me."

"Oh, and he knows you so well all of a sudden?"

"Well no, but you've got to admit we're pretty different. I mean, when it comes to sex anyway."

"Yeah, you do it more than I do, so what?"

"Well, that's what he was saying. He thought you were more, you know, open with your sexuality, he had no idea Brian was your first."

"You *told* him that?" a bolt of pain bores through my chest at the mention of Brian's name.

"I'm sorry dude, but it was getting really intense. Like, he really wanted to talk it out. He. He said that he never would have done what he did with you if he had had any inkling that it wasn't wanted. But that he just got this vibe from you, especially since you were so up for the reading and the body work and everything, that you wanted to experiment, that you wanted your life to change. He sees now that he totally misread it."

Hearing Janet quote Derek's slick, snappy lines flips a switch in my head, I'm starting to understand why Janet was so frustrated with *me*. I suddenly tear the paper off of my sandwich and take a big bite and the salt feels so good in my angry angry mouth and the juicy sounds of chewing echo in my head.

"I mean, most people don't take sex nearly as seriously as you do and that's sort of what we were talking about. Not that there's anything wrong with taking it seriously, but I just think about it really differently. And he told me how he's always admired that I'm not afraid of my sexuality. He used to watch me at work and he said he could just tell that I was strong and proud of my body. And it's true, you know? I've been so hung up on Lee lately that I haven't even slept with anyone in ages, not even just for fun."

"Janet, Jesus Christ, I can't believe you fell for his shit!"

"It's not shit. I *am* in touch with my sexuality, that's something I'm proud of. I love sex!"

"Sure, of course you do, but that's his game though, Janet, he talks you up so you're feeling so good that by the time he takes what he wants you're convinced he deserves it!" My lucidity is almost scaring me, but I can already hear creepy corners of my brain asking me if I have sexual dysfunction, if maybe I would have enjoyed Derek if I was normal, if I was like other girls. If I was like other girls, maybe Brian wouldn't have needed to cheat.

"Well, I know I shouldn't have slept with him, Kate, but not because I think that one-night-stands are sinful or anything. I shouldn't have slept with him because you're one of my best friends."

My heart goes wobbly for a minute. Best friends! I want this, I need this. But. "You still fucking did it though, Janet. I mean, do you know how much this man fucked up my life? After it was all over, when he kissed me that night, I thought this is it, he's going to rape me!" This hovers in the air for awhile and the Dagwood's women try to busy themselves again. "You slept with him, Janet. Knowing who he was." My voice cracks, I rub my eyes, I take another bite of my sandwich and it tastes like cement.

"I'm so sorry," says Janet through her snot and tears. "I make myself sick. That's the only word for it. I woke up Sunday morning and I felt completely sick. I don't know why I did it, Kate, I really don't. He just. He just made it seem like no big deal at all. Just sex. Just not being lonely for one night. He told me I was the most beautiful girl he'd seen in a long, long time and. It was so something I needed to hear. And when that night he came into the Cup, I felt like I had to act normal or he would think he was wrong about me, that I'm not what he thought I was. Oh my God, I sound so disgusting, I can't even believe myself. How will you ever forgive me?" She breaks down a little bit here, fat tears splash her sandwich.

Empathy kicks anger's ass for a minute and I know exactly why she did it. Fucking Derek. Another nubile notch on his belt. She could have been smarter, sure, she could have been nicer, yeah. But I can't stand that she felt bad enough to let him get to her. Janet! She was my rock. I look awkwardly at our Cokes in wax cups. Janet takes some breaths, twists a little piece of bun between her fingers and lays the yeasty knot beside the remainder of her bleeding sandwich. I feel like I've just stepped into one of those Funhouse rooms with a spongy floor at a cheap, dirty fair.

She takes my hand in hers, it's sticky with sub sauce. "Will you ever forgive me?" she asks, looking right into my eyes. I squeeze her fingers but then I take mine right back. I don't know what to do. I think of the muffins in my house, swollen huge with my wrath, I think of the past weekend, I think of how it's getting colder and I have no friends. I think about how if I was a different girl—the girl who Derek thought I was?—I wouldn't have minded what he did, I might have even taken an orgasm gladly, gone home feeling worldly and bored. I think about how that part of me *did* expect of Derek what he did and how I went to his place anyway, convinced myself that he would heal me, asked him point-blank for bodywork. I think about how Janet told me I had no hand in it and that he was nothing but a sleazy, horrid git and now she sits in front of me having kissed that git, having licked that git, that git who sits satisfied and pathetic in that varnished, empty place he inhabits alone. No. I don't know.

"I have to go back to work now," I say and push my chair back and walk out. From across the street, I shoot a glance back at Dagwood's and one of the sub-makers is comforting Janet. I shiver as I go back in the Cup, there is a wind blowing and it is getting harder.

"Hi," I say. I'm trembling. Visibly, I'm sure of it. Why did I do this? This guy called me a slut for Christ's sake, my mother would kill me if she knew I was here.

"Hi," says the old man. He looks somewhat bewildered,

somewhat annoyed. The TV talks and the cat pointedly ignores me. Or perhaps I'm being paranoid.

"I. I um. Brought you these muffins," I say and hand him eight of them in a baby-blue gift bag that I found in my closet. I am such a dork. "They're low-fat-banana-chocolate-chip," I squeak.

"Why did you bring me these?" the man asks, not unkindly. He's blinking like mad and wiggling his nose around again and it makes me want to do it too, but I hold myself back.

"Oh. Um. Because I feel badly. About last night I. I was having a bit of a temper tantrum I guess and I feel badly that I made all that noise and that. Well. I couldn't help but overhear that other guy saying he would phone the landlord and I guess I felt bad and I just wanted to let you know that if the landlord says anything, you can feel free to pass the blame on to me, just tell him to call me. Apartment three-o-four."

He's doing the head scratching thing now and he's laughing a little bit at the same time, holding the shiny blue bag in his non-scratching hand. "Yeah, I bet that'll work," he says, chuckling away. His voice is deep and friendly sounding, like Grandpas in laxative ads who have put their lives back on track.

"Well I guess I can leave my phone number with you if you think it'll be easier that way." What am I doing? Is this all a subconscious, elaborate suicide? A to-the-death game of Bait the Psycho?

"No no no," he says, his scratching stopped, "I'm just saying they won't believe me. Forget about it. Don't worry about it. I lost my temper too. Maybe he won't call this time."

"He's called before?"

"Oh yeah. Not just him. A bunch of others, too. I lose my temper, you know? You've heard it, don't act like you haven't heard it."

"Oh no. I've heard it," I say and then I look at my feet because of how bitchily I said this.

"Yeah. I know. Everybody hears it. I get angry sometimes," he says.

"About what?" I've looked up again, I'm looking at this man twitching his face and holding his muffins and I'm scared of him and I wish I wasn't and I'm starting to get really glad I came.

"I just get mad," he says. He looks annoyed, his hand looks ready to jump to his scalp, like he's using all the energy he has left to keep it down.

"I'm sorry," I say, "I didn't mean to pry. I just thought maybe I could—"

"What? Help?" he says. "What? Help?" he says again and it does not seem particularly normal that he has said it twice in a row. "I'm not interested in help. I'm fine just where I am," he says. It's still not unkind, but he's standing there with his arm all trembling, there's just something tense and electric going through him that I can't recognize or put into words and this indescribability of what is actually wrong is starting to freak me out and starting to make me stare. Just then the cat slides by me in that unbelievably sleek and subtle and sneaky way a cat could slide by anything.

"Ope. Your cat!" I say.

The old man's hand flies up, his fingers curl and frantically scratch away at his head. My so-glad-I-came bravado is quickly retreating, just as my body is stealthily beginning to do, one baby-step at a time.

"Fucking cat get the fuck back in here," the man says, loudly. Then he says it again, a little bit louder, then "fuck back in here, fuck back in here, fuck back in here," under his breath, his eyeballs slowly gravitating toward the fuzzy green "Murphy Brown" episode on the TV. The cat is lounging in a corner of the hallway, the hallway that twists in a sporadic and haunted way throughout the building. Not trying to get away, the cat is seemingly amused at the scene, perhaps pleased that this time it's my fault that she has inspired rage in her twitchy owner.

"Look, sorry I bothered you," I say. "I just wanted to apologize and let you know you could blame me fully and everything. I hope you like the muffins. They may be a little dry, I guess that's the low fat thing. But they're good microwaved. If you have a microwave."

"No bother. No bother," says the man.

As I wave and begin to leave, cooing at the cat and saying, "Go back to your daddy, go back honey-fur," I hear a crash, cast a glance back into the apartment and see that the old man is stomping one foot with all his might against the fake wood flooring.

"What the fuck? What the fuck? Shit cat." He yells and stomps and stomps.

I take a step back toward the door and he looks up at me and our eyes meet and I smile what I hope is a wide enough smile to counteract my plate-sized eyes and his eyebrows are going up and down at a dizzying rate and they are bushy and he is old and alone and just as I'm feeling sorry for him and wish I had brought him more food and maybe a mix tape he opens up his trembling mouth, wide, the top lip jumping up and to the left like someone's caught him with a fishing rod. "I'll kill you! I'll rape you! I'll love you!" he yells then, loud and clear and unmistakable and I suck in air that my lungs can't seem to process. Rape. That terror. Again. Again. I turn clumsily and start running down the hall. The cat is bristling in the corner and I hear the crash of his stomping and I hear the echo of his voice and those horrible horrible words and it doesn't sound like he's following but I won't look back because he might be and Christ, haven't I had enough? I run down the three flights of stairs, bolt out the door, run across the wide porch that links his building to mine, go thundering up my own three flights and lock myself into my apartment. I drag my desk up against the door and sit up on it and put my head in my hands and try to breathe and try to feel safe and try to hug myself, to love myself out of this crazy shit. It just doesn't work. I'm so scared again, but steelier this time. I want him out now, out out out, he's nothing but a sick fuck.

Of course Janet is more than happy to come over. I called her. I had to. Who else was I going to call? My parents? My mother would have hysterically driven the whole way here without stopping, careening through red lights she wouldn't notice. My father would have gripped the handle on the passenger side door until he was white-knuckled and might have timidly suggested she slow down slightly, until he remembered that his only daughter was in peril and he would have borne it with sweaty-palmed strength. I couldn't put them through that. Not after last weekend. Not ever.

I had to phone Janet. I couldn't leave the house, I was terrified he might be in my own creepy hallway, lurking round the corner, bristly like the cat. I couldn't even look out the window. What if he was looking out, staring at me, wearing his briefs, scratching his head, twitching his face, ready to pounce like some muddy, mangy carnivore lurking in the dark. I wish I knew Jimmy-from-downstairs's number, but we've only ever shared pleasantries when he carried my microwave upstairs, and besides he'd probably think I was hitting on him. It didn't really occur to me to phone the police, and when it finally did cross my mind, once I'd already called Janet, I was glad I hadn't. Forms to fill out, a need to be rational and coherent, these were things I would have been unprepared for, perhaps unable to execute, I'd probably freak out and it would end up being *me* committed to prison where I would sit, shaking and loveless until my trial where my old perverted neighbour would rant about my waking him up, shrieking about muffins and the death of the phallus.

So I phoned Janet. It can't be denied that a tiny part of me was pleased that circumstances had become so extenuating in so short a time that this call was necessary only one night after I had left her unforgiven at Dagwood's. She was so happy to hear my voice she practically whooped.

"Oh my God. Don't go anywhere. Stay right where you are, I'm coming right over," she said when I told her what had happened, "I have pepper spray. I'll be right there."

Pepper spray and Janet. I honestly can't wait. I hop off the desk I've been sitting on for the past hour and drag it away from the door again. I have a seat on my couch. I'm feeling remarkably calm now, though Janet's not here yet, I lean back against the cushions, remembering when I'd bought them on St. Denis during my first week here. I rest in this window of safety like an exploded, splintered raft, waterlogged and crusted with salt finally resting on a deserted beach. Potentially treacherous, but still. Rest. I look around my apartment and feel a sudden flood of adoration for it, its cracked walls that have held me through this, cradled me while I cried myself to sleep all these months away from home. These walls heavy with my postcard collection, a recycling schedule, a wallhanging my mom wove when she was a hippy. It's so different from the apartment I shared with Brian, so much more me. I've barely paid it any mind this whole time, and now its sanctuary status has taken a violent blow.

Janet arrives with a loud, "It's just me," and four solid knocks. I open the door and she stands in front of me, her face screwed up into a ridiculous detectivish squint. When she sees me, this wilts a bit, I see her guilt shine through but she maintains an air of determination. She is wielding her tiny can of pepper spray, around her elbow she has her little pink purse and a backpack bulges behind her. She clearly wants to save my life.

"He's not out here," she says and bites her lower lip.

"Come in," I say.

She does. Once we've closed and locked the door again she starts to look at her feet and her face becomes Jello-like. She apparently has no idea what sort of expression a regretful back-stabber should assume and her confused facial muscles just wiggle around uncomfortably under her pale, pretty skin.

"I. Um. I brought some pajamas and stuff in case you wanted me to stay. I mean, just if you were scared or whatever."

"Yeah. That would be cool," I say. "Did you bring your uniform?"

"Uh huh. I'll just go to work straight from here and you can come with, that way we can walk out together."

"Okay," I say. Of course! There's tomorrow. And a next day. And a lot more days that I have to live across the fire escape from this man. Will Janet have to move in, stand guard with the pepper spray?

Of course seeing her reminds me of Derek. And her and Derek. And me and Derek. But I don't want to think about it tonight. I smile brightly. I thank her for coming. I am truly thankful. She looks so relieved and thunks down onto my yellow rug, starts unzipping her backpack out of which springs a sleeping bag, microwave popcorn, a bag of fruit, some bagels, a brick of cheese and a bottle of Jaegermeister.

"I figured we'd need some supplies," she says to me, tossing me some shy eye contact and a smile.

"Very nice," I say.

"Wanna drink?" she asks.

"Hell yeah," I say and watch Janet bustle into the kitchen to pour us shots.

An hour later we're drunk. Janet is half in her sleeping bag on the rug and I'm curled on the couch. We keep trading each other the cheese and a knife for the bottle of Jaegermeister.

"What a fucking fucker," Janet is slurring. "I can't believe he kissed you. What an asshole."

"I know," I say, slicing off a chunk of cheese. I've told her of my weekend in Toronto, I didn't mean to, but after two shots it was just irresistible and I began to tell all. It's almost like a rebirth I'm thinking now, so many shots later, my brain soft and gooey, my legs like noodles overcooked. This is just like it was when I first met Janet, we went out and got trashed and I told her about my little egg man. My little asshole.

"I know. He's such an asshole, Janet, and that's the thing. Like I hear you say that? And I know that's true, you know? But I just. I still can't really believe it, you know? Like I'm still. Part of me's still just so convinced that he's the most perfect man in the world."

Janet sits bolt upright and then slides a bit on the slippery synthetic fabric of her sleeping bag.

"Katy," she says regally, "he's not. He's an asshole."

We look at each other, sharing drunk logic, convinced of our profundity and I pass Janet the cheese and she passes me the bottle and I relish the perfect burn as it slides into my insides and I wag my heavy, heavy head around and catch sight of the desk we pushed against the door again. The sleepy butterflies in my belly give a couple of urgent flaps but I don't want to deal with it. Janet's here. Everything's okay.

"Janet," I say, "why do we date assholes? Like, Lee is an asshole, too. Why do we spend all our time letting our worth be defined by assholes?" I feel like my life has become a crappy knock-off of an Atwood novel.

"Lee didn't even date me. At least with Brian you got to go through a real genuine, like, heartbreak. From something real. Not just getting a random dryhump from behind."

"Yeah. That's true. But honestly, right now, I would trade in all the good so I didn't have to feel this shitty."

"No way. No, you wouldn't. You have that forever, that kind of stuff. Like. Like when you guys were first together, stuff you told me about, like when you went to Toronto Island that time. When you told me about that, you were just fucking glowy."

"Yeah," I say and I can feel it, I'm fucking glowy all over again, thinking of that hot, hot day, wearing barely any clothes at all, feeling Brian's fingers on my arm on the ferry over, him touching my nose-ring on the sky-ride, this ski-lift that goes nowhere, just around and around above the lake and the farm and the amusement park for tiny, happy children.

"You wouldn't want to give that up," Janet says, her mouth full of cheese, sliding back down into her makeshift bed.

"We were so sweaty that day," I say, still lost in the memory, "that we tasted really salty that night. It made us laugh really hard. We licked each other's arms."

"Hot," says Janet and I see she doesn't get it and no one will, I need to keep these memories, even if they are just mine and Brian's, even if they're just mine, even if I'm just drunk, I want them, I want them forever. I just wish they wouldn't saw through me every time I hang out with them, but that's what they do and I feel it now, too, thinking of Brian's laughing face, tongue on my elbow, it gives me a physical pain in my chest and I don't understand how this can be when the heart is just a trope, an ancient one at that. How can a metaphor feel so real? I take another drink and when I put the bottle down, Janet's face is all twisted up again.

"I'm so sorry about what I did," she says, and she is crying and she walks on her knees to where I am on the couch and she puts her head in my lap and I put my hand on her shiny brown hair.

"I'm so so sorry," she sobs. "I don't know what kind of a sick person I am, I don't know. I just. It was the stupidest night ever. I just wish that Lee hadn't…"

I'm patting her head. "You're in love with Lee, aren't you?"

She nods into my leg and keeps crying a little bit and I stroke her hair, full of alcohol, forgiveness and cheese. And suddenly I hear a grunt. Then another one, harsh and animalistic. A strangled scream. Janet's head snaps up from my lap, she clumsily gets to her feet, stumbles around for the pepper spray. I'm hit with the white light of sudden sobriety that only fear can cause. I curl my legs underneath me, trying to shrink. Janet has gone to inspect the bathroom, then the kitchen and in this moment I don't find it ludicrous. The grunting doesn't stop. It's almost rhythmic. Who is screaming? My heart has lost all sense of dignity, it's banging away, trying to get out and make a run for it.

"It gets louder when I'm in the kitchen," says Janet, coming back into the main room.

"That's where the window is," I say, trying not to move at all, pretending I'm not here.

"Yeah." Her detective face has resurfaced. "But it sounds like it's coming from below."

We listen again, closely. Janet puts her ear to my rug.

Slowly, I get off the couch and follow suit.

"Grunt grunt," says the floor. And then, "Ahhhahh-hhahhh!"

And then, "Yes! Oh God."

I look at Janet and she's already laughing. "Somebody's *fucking*," she lolls and my drunkenness returns as quickly as it retreated. I let out a guffaw, I giggle, I can't stop. It's just Jimmy from downstairs. Grunting away. I absently realize I haven't even masturbated in months and I make a mental note to take it up again after a particularly loud scream from below.

"Lucky lady," Janet hoots, and we lie chortling on the rug and listen till they're done.

The next day Janet goes to work and I leave with her because I don't want to be in the apartment alone. Our hangovers pound between us as we walk down Ste. Catherine. Every day it feels colder and smells fresher like the rot and fetid sweat of the summer is being blown out at the city-wide cost of having to wear a jacket and socks. Fall and my hangover tighten screws in my brain and I've decided that when I get home tonight I'm going to call the landlord myself and discuss The Incident as I will call it. I will see what can be done in a civil, grown up way. Also, Janet and I have decided to go out more.

"I think we spend too much time at work and not enough time dancing," I'm saying.

"Yeah, we should go out this weekend."

"Yeah!" I say, rapturous that she is on the same page. "Meet us some men!"

"I thought you were sick of being defined by assholes," Janet smirks.

"Shit, the next one is gonna be defined by *me!*" I say loudly, with much mock-sass and by the time I've dropped her off at the Cup, she has suggested an electronic music event at the Societé des arts technologiques she read about in the paper and I have agreed to go completely, lock stock and barrel whole hog one hundred percent even though I generally don't get electronic music and anything called an event tends to intimidate the dance out of me. But we're going. We will go. And now, head bonging with Jaegermeister memories I decide to go to the Y to try to purge myself of anything evil left lurking and I compose sentences from a distance about how I've been a total emotional bulimic lately, binging on nostalgia and jealousy and tears and then feeling better, so much better than a person should feel and convincing myself that this is the last time. Well *this*, I think, is the very last time. It's time this madness stopped.

At the gym I decide to take a class called Muscle Toning Express, impressed by the title's suggestion of a fast fix. It's taught by a lovely lady named Julie. The whole thing is in French which I figure is a fringe benefit and I am very keen in my Zeller's yoga pants and a green tank top. Julie's got the Madonna pumping and I look at myself in the wall of mirrors noting that when I do my squat my spine makes a nice long, curved line and my bum sticks out round and cute just like Julie's.

About fifteen minutes later I am a ruddy glob of gelatinous sweat and raspy inhalations yanking on elasticized tubing wrapped around my trembling quads.

"*Huit! Sept! Six! Cinq!*" screams Julie. She was so friendly before. Now she's a peppy little goblin with a saccharin smile stuck on like a bad brooch.

"*Et un autre huit!*"

I lie on my back and giggle mirthlessly. The supposedly motivational music asks if I know what it feels like for a girl? In this world? This is the third time the song has been played. Julie apologized five minutes in, explaining that she brought the CD single instead of the regular one by mistake. This is the only song we've got.

This particular exercise studio, Studio Four, has wall-length windows on one side that face onto the conditioning room where all the weight-lifting machines and men are. As one guy walks past, on his way from one machine to another, his outsized bulges glistening in the tube lighting, he casts a glance into Studio Four. A glance that scathes and appraises and rates and berates all at the same time. Just a glance, just a brief pause, cracks a small, haughty smile through the wall of glass. I imagine how we look to him, pumping our legs up and down, squatting in unison, puffy and red-faced. Do you know? What it feels like? For a girl? I nail him with a dirty look through the glass, but just as I narrow my eyes, something yanks them, hard, to the far end of the gym. I stop moving for a second, convinced that I'm hallucinating due to too many glute-squats, but no, there he is, even after a cartoon double take, the old man from my building, mopping a section of the stretching area.

I can barely pay attention for the last eighty-five thigh

busters, let alone exhale on the up, inhale on the down, but I don't want the class to end. I can't go out there. His mopping moves him steadily toward Studio Four and when at last we all applaud and thank Julie and put our mats away, he is maybe fifteen feet from the door.

I push my way into the conditioning room, keeping my back to him but my stupid shock of bleached hair betrays me every time. He has seen me. He is doddering toward me, wielding his mop. Part of me knows that nothing can happen, we're in public, the most he can do is threaten me again. I don't want to be threatened, I don't want extra ammo to tell the landlord, I just want to be left the hell alone. So I run. I start running toward the doors that lead to the stairs that lead to the change rooms and I'm dodging muscley men and elliptical trainers and a woman in a red staff jacket bellows at me to get on the track. So I do. But I keep running. I scoot through one of the openings in the fence that separates the track from the equipment and I run and run and run as fast as I can and I can't stop. Because the old man is following me. I can't believe he has this kind of endurance, but he's been behind me the whole time, I can hear his breathing, harsh and raspy but steady and I think of dirty phone calls and I miss the gap in the fence that would lead me to the out-doors and I say "shit" and check behind me, and there he is, shaking his dripping mop and I keep running and he does too and I'm so worn out and I feel so dumb and I don't know what to do, yell rapist? Yell madman? And I run and run and run and then he catches me.

"Ah!" I squeal and stop dead because there's weight on my shoulder and it's his old and liver-spotted hand and he's leaning on me trying to catch his breath and I'm incredulous because what gives him the fucking right and I don't push him away because this is among the weirdest things that's ever happened to me. It's certainly the fastest I've ever run.

"I wanted to..." he wheezes, disengaging from my shoulder and straightening up. We walk to the side of the track and I stare at him, making sure the red-jacketed woman is in my sightline.

"I wanted to," he begins again, "apologize. For yesterday."

"Oh?" This surprises me somewhat though I had no idea what to expect. But I somehow thought it would be harsher and more deranged.

"I. Sometimes... have no... control over... the things I say," he says, still trying desperately to breathe normally. I notice that he seems less twitchy than yesterday, one hand holds the mop, the other hangs loose at his side.

"I say things, the exact things, that I know are wrong," he tells me.

"No kidding," I say. "Why the hell would you say that to me? Do you have any idea how scared I was?"

"I don't know. I can't help it."

My neighbour can't help but threaten to rape and kill. What do you say to that?

"It happens when I'm stressed or nervous. It's like when I scratch my head. I can't stop it, I can't. When I yell at Petunia too."

"Petunia?" I can smell the old man, he's sweaty and it makes me queasy.

"My cat."

"Oh."

"Sometimes I'm just mad. But sometimes it's different. If I don't do it… if I don't say things. Well. It's just not an option. Like yesterday, this is what I'm trying to tell you, I would never want to scare a young woman like yourself."

Although I'm trying to have a nice strong guard up, mentally preparing myself to knee him in the balls, referring to me as a young woman breaks my heart a little bit.

"Well you did. You really did scare me." I try to give him a look that says I'm willing to hear more.

"I'm. I know that it would be very frightening for me to say that I'm going to rape you or kill you. Or even love you for that matter, that's what," and here he starts to scratch his head and his face buckles, "that's just the opposite of what I was trying to say to you, you understand, I. I thought it was awfully nice of you to bring those muffins by. And I was having a bad day and. That's what happens. Just when I want to say 'thank you, thank you for stopping by' exactly what I don't want to say comes out."

It seems that it's almost physically painful for him to tell me about this, he's scratching a bit more furiously now, looking down and to the side, twitching his nose. He is not well. I know that he's not, I've known since I moved in and heard him screaming in the mornings.

"I would like to buy you lunch if you would let me," he says then, to the rubberized track, "to make amends for having frightened you, nothing more. Nothing more." He murmurs "nothing more" a few more times to himself, then wrenches his head up and looks at me.

"To make amends," he says again and his hand comes down and hovers at his side. I look around me, all these people oblivious to this bizarre thing that is transpiring, necks bulging as they lift and lower and repeat. "I finish my shift in fifteen minutes," he says, nodding at the mop.

"Sure," I say. "That'll give me time to take a shower."

"I'm going to need one, too," says the old man. "I fucking reek."

I smile. "I'm Kate."

He reaches out his hand that shakes a bit. "John. I'll meet you at the entrance in twenty minutes?"

We begin our walk to the Place des Arts St. Hubert in relative silence. From time to time John scratches his head and I pretend not to notice but I want to know what it is. I feel like I'd be a lot more calm if the whole thing had a name. I chat a bit about the weather and he nods and agrees and even smiles when I say that our apartment complex is a smelly death oven. Then I feel guilty for bringing it up because he's old and should be living comfortably. For me squalor is a necessary and transitional phase of my initiation into adulthood. We are going to St. Hubert even though it's a twenty minute walk from the Y because he gets an employee discount and he has to work at three o'clock.

"You have two jobs?" I ask, hoping my incredulity hasn't cracked through the sunny mask of forgiveness I've been affecting since we left the Y.

"Yeah, yeah, I bus tables there, do some dishes, that sort of thing. Just part time, you know. Plus they have the best coleslaw in the entire world," he says.

"Yeah, I share that sentiment whole-heartedly," I say. "I mean the coleslaw. I used to go to St. Hubert with my parents all the time. I used to get a chicken drumstick meal with a glass of milk. It kicked ass." I am suddenly hyper-conscious of my youthful vernacular. I feel like a bad actor with a bad script.

"*This* St. Hubert?" John is scratching his head again but I think I'm getting more successful at not flinching.

"No, no. In Toronto."

"Toronto?" John's brow is furrowed, his nose atwitch.

Oh oh. I get a shot of adrenaline. What if the mention of our country's most hated city sets off another rape and kill tirade?

"Yeah. I just moved here this summer actually."

"They have St. Hubert in *Toronto*?"

"Oh yeah. Well, in the suburbs mostly."

"Well I'll be damned," John gives a few satisfied nods. "I really woulda thought it was only in Quebec."

Man. I have to relax. I mean, this guy chased me through the Y to tell me he's sorry. He's not going to kill me. Not at St. Hubert. We pass the Musée d'art contemporain where Derek and I went and I look right at it without feeling sick. The sun shines down, the breeze gossips about the months to come and I'm walking down the street with this twitchy old man. Is this not the stuff of which epiphanies are made? I breathe in the fresh air and we wait for the light to change.

The St. Huberts are so slick and happening here in the province of their birth compared to the yellow vinyl upholstery and the humbly obscure locations of the Toronto branches. The place is packed at one PM on a Tuesday, the lighting is hip, the decor is modern and fast French bubbles all around us.

A red haired hostess whisks us in after John has exchanged pleasantries with her in French. She nods dismissively at his attempts at conversation and I pretend to be fascinated by the specials board so that he won't think I noticed. We follow the hostess through the huge main room, past the sprawling bar. John gives a charming smile, he barely twitches at all. He twinkles his eyes at me in an almost unnervingly grandfatherly manner and I wonder for the first time if he's as weirded out by all of this as I am, if he's improvising too. We are finally seated in one of the smaller, upstairs areas, near the bathrooms. There is no one else in this section. John doesn't seem to notice.

"You know," he says proprietorially, "even though I work here, I still love coming in."

"Yeah, it's tasty!" I say.

"So's that waitress!" He laughs a hoarse old man laugh and I'm pretty sure he even says "great ass" under his breath just before it devolves into a coughing fit followed by a few low-volume "fucks".

I stare at him blatantly this whole time, afforded this luxury by the traditional arrangement of the table-for-two. He is wearing a dark grey, long-sleeved golf shirt tucked into a pair of green, twill pants, pulled up high and belted. He looks like he might have been handsome, but the twitching and the rage have taken their toll. His face is droopy, pale, ashy, his grey hair wild and wiry. He has crazy eyes that one minute can do that grandfather thing and the next minute flash fury. Or confusion. Or pain. I haven't known him long enough to separate these three.

"Christ almighty," he says at the end of the coughing and the swearing. "What are you going to get to eat?"

"Um."

"Have anything you want," he says, suddenly sweeping his arm dramatically across the plasticized menu. "The ribs, whatever. I get the discount for both of us."

"Oh. Thanks," I say. "I think I'll just go with the quarter chicken Quick Lunch."

"That's it?" he says.

"Yeah, well it comes with an ice cream."

"Sure, whatever you like."

He orders for both of us when the waitress arrives.

"Okay," she says curtly, her pencil making a scraping noise as she writes down his hot chicken sandwich and my side dish choices. She barely looks up from her pad.

"Wow, friendly service," I say in spite of myself after she leaves.

"Ah, she's just pissed off cause I called her fatso this one time. Told her she had big, fat, black ass." He almost whispers these things when he says them. Then he folds his hands in front of him and looks at his nails.

"Why would you say that?" I ask.

"I told you, I say the wrong thing sometimes," he tells me with annoyance at the edges as if we've known each other for decades, as if he tells me this daily.

"Yeah but. I mean really. Can't you... I mean, when you're at work? Like, control it?"

"If I could, don't you think I would?" he snaps, then softens. "I try. I apologized to her." He is looking out the window onto Ste. Catherine, his shoulder is bouncing with no apparent rhythm. "They know I'm sick, you know. They all know. They leave me alone." These things come out of his mouth like pop from a shaken can, all at once, loud, disorganized. "They always think at first that they're the nice ones, at every new job everybody thinks that they're the ones who'll be nice to the old sick guy and then they all hate me in the end because I always say something. I can't help it. But they all know. So they can't can me right away, you know? Not from washing the dishes." He doesn't look overly upset when he tells me this, it's as if he just wants me to understand, to know that *he* knows, that he's not blind to their stares. Neither am I. I see two of the waitresses whispering, pointing at me from the alcove with the computer and the coffee pot. They wonder who I am, why I'm here. I wonder, too, I don't know how to feel.

"If you're sick, why don't you get help?" I say, just the very minute that some of the better parts of my brain have gotten together and decided that that's a bullshit none-of-my-business thing to say, but then it's too late. Those better parts of my brain back down, defeated and leave the nosey-parker part exposed and ashamed.

"Help help help. That's nothing. There's no such thing as help," he says, waving his hands around in a little dance. There is another bout of headscratching, I try to look away and then our food arrives. The waitress thunks down John's hot chicken sandwich so hard the gravy jiggles, then offers me a terse smile with my meal. I give her one back and she walks away.

"That was fast," I say, wanting to change the subject from "help", wishing I'd never brought it up.

"Oh yeah, they run a tight ship in that kitchen," says John, grinning and spearing about six fries on his fork. He pours himself out a sizable gob of ketchup, dips the fries in, then proceeds to mash them around in the gravy on top of his chicken sandwich. Finally he pops the sodden mass into his mouth, proclaiming "yes" as he begins to chew.

With his mouth still slightly full and his other hand already engaged in repeating the fry process, John asks me if I moved here for school.

"Just kind of wanted to get out of Toronto."

"Hm. You had some trouble in Toronto?"

I have a vague idea that "trouble" to John's generation means only one thing.

"I wasn't pregnant," I say.

"Well? What was it then? Why does a young girl like you move all the way to a foreign part of the country? There must've been some kind of trouble." He repeats the word trouble under his breath but it becomes intermingled with something resembling a chuckle. He seems to enjoy this gossiping and he most definitely is enjoying the hot chicken sandwich which he is currently slicing into tiny, square pieces.

"Dentures, you know?" he says when he notices me staring at his handiwork. "So? Really. Why did you move? Must have something to do with that man."

"What man?" A little earthworm of fear wriggles through me again, I wonder if maybe he's been stalking me, what if he thinks this is a date—

"Ryan? Brian? That fellow you were caterwauling about the other night, so loud nobody could stand it."

Oh, right. I keep forgetting that half the reason I'm here today is that I also lack control over what I say and at what volume and I have no medical justification for this behaviour. I rend a piece of chicken with my fork, dunk it in the St. Hubert sauce and spear up some fries as well.

"Ex-boyfriend," I say. John looks at me as he chews, his face still wrenching around even as he eats, his scratching hand jiggling at his side, his head nodding sporadically up and down.

"Was he good in the sack?" John asks.

I nearly snarfle coleslaw up my nose and have to have a sip of my milk but then I say, "Yeah." It's a valid question.

"But you left him?"

"I'd thought we would get back together when I moved back home in a year or so."

"Did ya? You just thought he'd take you back after you up and left him." He says this kind of playfully, shaking a coleslaw-glutted fork in my direction.

"Sounds dumb. But… we had this connection."

"I understand. Connection." John pops a cubic centimetre of chicken sandwich into his mouth. "You probably wanted everything to go your way all the time and when it didn't, you got pissed off and left. Am I right?" He's mashing fries around again, with a bit more hostility than before. So far this is less epiphanic than I'd hoped.

"He cheated on me."

"Let me guess, you two had been together awhile, you thought it was getting serious," he says now, looking right at me with his inscrutable eyes. I can't say that he looks angry, but I'm worried that these are the eyes of the John whose distorted subconscious dupes his voice into calling me a slut and racializing women's asses. I am sure that this is the old man who scares the hell out of me. "Maybe you shared an apartment? And you always wanted him at home. Right?"

"No. No I didn't. We had really independent lives actually."

"But I bet you wanted him home for dinners. Or if he wasn't coming, you wanted him to call first?"

"Why are you asking me that?" This is starting to freak me out a little bit and I'm finding it less and less endearing to watch him make his food denture friendly.

"I'm just guessing," he says, loosening his tone a bit, "that's just what these things are usually like, you know, women can just be so goddamned demanding, that's all I'm saying."

"Demanding? Is it so demanding to want someone to call if they're not going to show up on time when you've been cooking forever? Or to want a surprise from time to time? Or some indication that you actually matter?"

"Oh, here we go. See this is what I'm telling you, it's always the same goddamn story. A surprise! Give me a break. No wonder."

"No wonder what? No wonder he cheated on me? Jesus Christ. I thought we came here to make amends! Isn't that what you said? I thought you were done insulting me." I'm getting a little bit heated and I can feel chicken sticking in between my molars. I'm trying to keep my voice down, but I have a sneaking suspicion I'm failing.

"Hey, don't get your panties in a twist there, Kate," chuckling again, "I just think sometimes it's not the worst thing to look at the other side of the coin for a change, you know? I mean, here's a guy right? Virile, young, energetic. He never wanted to fall in love. Then he meets you. You hit it off, the sex is great—"

"Look, just for*get* the sex." I don't know why, but every time he says the word it makes me stab my chicken's thigh.

"Sure, everything's great. Suddenly, you're asking him to do everything with you. Am I wrong? All of the sudden, he's going to your family weddings and all this kind of shit with you and he's wondering what's going on and he's still really enjoying himself, sure, so it's okay. And in the meantime, he's started telling you all his personal baggage and everything, like what makes him tick, right? Like, what's really underneath it all or whatever. Why? Because you keep asking. That's what you do, you women, you just ask ask ask. Questions all the fucking time." And now it's him who's having trouble with his volume and his hand has flown up again to scratch his head and I imagine that it's greasy and that grosses me out and it really really pisses me off that he is reducing me to "you women" as if we are some team of vacuous clones cookie-cuttered out of the doughy remnants of the stronger sex.

"You don't know what you're talking about," I say and stare him down. "You have no idea. How could you when all you do is sit in your weird little apartment with your mangy little cat and scratch your head all day without even giving a shit that you're crazy as fuck?"

"I am NOT crazy!" he yells this, then calms right down. Immediately. He's breathing deeply, I can see it, I can see his soft, old lips mouthing numbers, one two three... The waitress who served us has bee-lined over to ask if everything's all right and I shock myself when I tell her that everything's just fine, that we were just joking around. She looks unconvinced, probably because I do, but she leaves us alone.

"I'm sorry," I say. "You're just really pissing me off. You know? I mean, you don't even know me. Or Brian. Then you sit there and tell me how I fucked it up? I mean, I don't have to take that."

"I'm not crazy."

"I know. It's a disease." I don't know. I have no idea.

"It's a syndrome," he says with a dramatic wriggle of his nose. "I have an acute case. Tourette's Syndrome. It is only accompanied by random outbursts of filth in ten percent of the cases, but that's what makes it such a popular syndrome with the media." He has affected some kind of reedy, journalistic drawl. "Tourette's Syndrome is characterized by both physical and mental tics, it is often accompanied by obsessive thoughts and behaviours and is treatable with drugs and counselling. That's what my wife told me. That's what she found out."

"You have a wife?"

"I did. Then it got all messed up. That's what I'm saying. Every story's the same. You tell a woman too much, it'll all go wrong. You have to get away."

"But she was trying to help you!" I can't believe him. This disgusts me, this misogyny, this clichéed cantankerous old fart gumming down his chicken, talking shit about his estranged wife.

"Help like hell. All she wanted was for me to fix it. Thought I could just fix it. 'You have to fight this, John,' she said it all the time. All the time. Therapy this and anti-depressants that and new research, new drugs, new everything. She just wanted to stick me full of electrodes and blast me. Just like all the rest. Just the same, my whole life, that's what they did when I was a kid, that's what they'd do again now. You have to get away from that. You have to. Live your own fucking life. That's what I'm saying. It's always the same. You get too close, they take it from you."

"They don't even use electro-shock therapy any more!" I say. How can he be so exasperating? How can he not see that she was just trying to love him? She was just doing what was right? Not just for her. For him, too. For them!

"Oh, they use it! They do! They get you on the other stuff first, so you don't even know it's going to happen, but I know they'd do it again if they got a chance."

"Christ, John, you left your wife because she wanted to help you? Is that what you're telling me?"

"I left her because you have to. It can't work, it doesn't work. I had to leave because she made me leave."

"She left you then."

Silence.

"She would have stayed if you'd worked on it, gotten help?"

"Shut up about help. Jesus. You try to have a decent lunch, but you see? Even now! Questions, questions all the time. It never stops with women."

"This is so sad."

"What?"

"This! This! All of it. This is crazy, John, don't you see that you—that things could have been so different for you?

145

You don't have to work here. Or at the Y. You could have—"

"I could have! I could have what? Where else would hire me, huh? I had plenty of other jobs but I got fired from every single one of them because I told some jerk in the mailroom he was a pizza-face or I called some secretary a slutty cunt and they don't give a shit when you're working with people around you that it's a syndrome or a disease or anything. It just doesn't look right. It isn't right. So I'm out."

"But she tried to help you!" I can't help but yell this, I want the volume to make it penetrate, to drill it into his thick, crazy hair, through his spotty scalp into his old, old brain, to make him think.

"She did try," he says, "she tried her goddamn hardest. And the harder she tried the more I wanted her not to know me any more. The more I wanted to go away. From everything." There's gravy on his twitching lips.

"But that's not her fault!"

"All I'm saying is that this Brian guy's probably better off where he's at now."

"But John! That's not the same fucking story! I didn't try to do anything. I just loved him. That's all. And he didn't love me back! Not enough anyway. That's all it was."

"Yeah? Then how come you're still up screaming about it at all hours of the night?"

"Because it hurts!"

"Why, because some asshole who never even told you he loved you isn't with you anymore? Because you can't wait up at night for him to call you like he said he would and then just cry all over your pillow instead? Because you don't have that constant knot of fear in your stomach all the time that maybe he's going to dump you today, maybe he's met someone else?"

"How do you know he never told me he loved me? God! You don't know shit."

"Sure I do. Shit is one thing I know plenty about, I've seen plenty of it. I put my wife through plenty of it, too. You know what? She let it get to her, too. Sad all the goddamn time. If she'd just have let it go. If she could have just let me be instead of trying to save my fucking life."

"You asshole."

"Well. Yes. I suppose I can be one of those sometimes." This makes me laugh. I can't help myself. It makes him laugh, too, and we even make eye-contact in the middle of it. But once the laughing subsides, I have no idea what to say. We both finish what's left of our lunches, I mop up all my sauce with my toasted bun.

"This was really delicious," I say.

"Glad you liked it," he says, shakily wiping gravy from the corners of his mouth. "I'm sorry if I got carried away."

"Yeah. Me, too, I think."

Just then my ice cream arrives. I gallantly ask for an extra spoon. "Wanna split it?" I ask.

"No," he says, shaking his head. "I have to get ready for work. I'll pay on my way."

He leaves me sitting alone at the table for two in the only empty section in the place.

At home, things have a new lustre. Not a bright, super-shiny lustre, but a fuzzy, matte one that reminds me that I am not condemned to live in fear. I move my desk from beside the door to its original spot against the wall. I look out the window onto the network of fire escapes that connect the two buildings. Mine and John's. And how many others. Maybe five per floor? Three floors per building. Fifteen people? Maybe two to an apartment in a few of them, the slightly bigger ones. All of us living with slanted floors and Lilliputian kitchens and all of us with something stuck up on the wall, or nothing at all. All stacked on top of each other and stuck into this street, between other buildings, like a Playmobil town, just little pieces of Montreal. Today. Just right now. I'm in bed with my yellow comforter pulled up under my chin, I've taken my pants off and I'm rubbing my feet together and the sheets are cool and there's a stiff little breeze coming in through the window and I wonder about John's wife, if she's still alive, if she ever loved again. Did they have kids? Why didn't I ask? Will I have a chance to ask again? Are we friends or do I hate him? Were the kids infested with the syndrome, too? Is it hereditary? Did he not let them have drugs either? The kids would be all grown up. Where do they live? Where is their love? Where does it go? I'm thinking of them as I drift away to dreams and I don't even notice the huge significance of this, the staggering departure from the globby Brian-fog of the last few weeks the last few months the last few years, instead I just fall down into sleep's soft, gnarled hands that keep me and rock me and squeeze me so hard.

I sling coffee the next three days, all day long, can I help who's next please, is that skim or regular, sweetener's on the table, yep in the middle, it has a shot of banana syrup in it and half a shot of vanilla, no, no, that's my fault, I'm sorry, let me get you another one, regular or large, no that's our regular there is no small, yes silly I know, look I didn't write the menu, no I'm sorry, no it's only Tuesdays that that's on special, Isabelle is it my break next, well sorry for asking, fuck Janet I'm gonna eat my own arm off, I know, they never motherfuckin tip, do you think they know how little we make, yes, sorry, I'll tuck in my shirt I just forgot, yeah, I think it's a good flavour, yeah I've tried them all, *oui, oui, parlez-vous, non, desolé*, Janet can you do this, my French sucks today, I'm going to go do refills, yeah I'll do the tables first, sure, sure no problem, sure sure, I reek, I reek, I fucking reek of coffee, and. It's. Friday.

Finally. I have tomorrow off. Tonight Janet and I are going out. I am positively jovial. I'm going to get dressed up, I'm going to wear lipstick, I'm going to dance, maybe we'll even talk to people we've never talked to before.

At home I put on some Prince and shake it a little as I wriggle out of my whipped cream crusted pants and my limp golf shirt that hasn't been washed in three weeks. I dance around in just my socks right in front of my full length mirror and allow myself that sliver of a moment, come on, you've all had one, even if it was just a tiny one—have you all had one?—where I see my body as young and perfect and beautiful and my little breasts bounce up and down and my hilarious bum jiggles around and my tummy is round and my bleach job is bad and I'm cute, dammit! Dammit Brian, you are missing out—SHHHHHH! Not tonight. Tonight he's not there, not in my mirror, not in my mind and suddenly there's John, wailing away at Petunia and I wrench my window open and wrap my naked self in my long blue curtain and stick my head right out into the chasm.

"Hey John, why don't you just leave that cat alone for a change? Huh?"

And he bounds right out through his crappy screen door and stands out on his part of the fire escape in nothing but a green and sagging pair of briefs and bellows out into the cool early evening, "Because I get angry sometimes!" and he sees my head poking out the window and we look at each other and he's such a mean, gross old guy, standing there fat and sagging and scratching but he smiles a bit when he sees it's me and I stick out my arm and give a little wave.

"Aw, you just... leave me be," he says and goes back muttering and I watch him bang around in his kitchen and I think that maybe, just maybe he's getting Petunia a cat treat and I pull my head back into my own place so that I can believe forever that he did and that this day is as big and round and golden and full of heat as the fat Fall sun slipping down behind our buildings, leaving behind the cool, fizzy potential energy of fresh darkness.

When we walk in the place is really well lit and there's a mirror on the wall and I look good. Really good. I actually like the music, I feel like I can really relate to it in some way and Janet looks terrific and we walk up to the bar to get some drinks and this guy, I swear, right away, as if from heaven swoops down and starts talking to Janet. And then. Then. HE walks up to the bar. He says "hey" to the dude Janet's talking to and smiling at and laughing with and I'm so happy and proud of her but all of the sudden I can't breathe any more because of this other guy. He's gorgeous. He's shy. He looks at his feet that are in beautiful sneakers, I look at his legs that are in sexy sexy worn out jeans, my God he dresses like he's from Toronto the lascivious heathen part of my brain blasphemes. He's wearing a soft t-shirt and he starts to talk to me. He's funny and a little bit drunk already and he asks if he can buy me a drink, if that jives with my politics. AND! He has a little French accent. But there's so not enough of a language barrier that it impedes our exchange of witty *bons mots* and I tell him it's cool, he can buy me a beer and he digs how I want beer and not some huge, expensive mixed drink with a swizzlestick and limes. We stand close to each other and talk about books at first and then about movies and about the music that's playing and then about nothing at all really, just laughs and excitement and wide-eyed enthusiasm about all the stuff that no one else in the world ever gets so excited about—like wiener dogs!—because he gets me—I can tell!—and there's a hot feeling between our thighs and I want to take him home right away, but I don't and we get drunk and we dance and we talk and we laugh some more and out of the corner of my eye I see Janet doing the same thing with her hot new man and at the end of the night the boy and I share a cab and we share our numbers on little pieces of paper torn from stuff we desperately search for in our pockets, mine on a matchbook, his on a chunk of a cigarette box—he smokes!—and he touches my hair and tells me how nice it was to meet me and I say, "same here" and I look down and feel a little bit dumb after he leaves the cab that I said something as suburban as "same here", but it is so nice to dwell on, such a perfect twinge of fear and pain and longing and joy because he will be it and I am ready, hooray, I have taken a big old running start at the springboard and now I've jumped, now I've landed, now I've come down and whump! Brian Johnson has been bounced right out of the stratosphere and I am strolling away from this so pretty, so unscathed, so wise and worthy with his number in my pocket and my very own apartment in this rad bilingual city full of cool cool shit.

Yeah so what if that was just a fantasy blamming through my head and really I'm still in the shower exfoliating and shaving and plucking, there is no reason I can't make this happen, there is absolutely no reason it won't.

I pick up Janet from her place, I mean for real this time, and we walk the twenty minutes giggling and ready in cloppy heels and short skirts and eyes all aglitter with Maybelline and desire. When we walk in there is a really long line for the coat check. And the place is dark. Very loud and dark. There's a couple in a corner wearing all black, the girl is wearing a black leather tie and they are making out against the wall and they're holding each others' hands up above their heads. I get this uncanny feeling that Janet and I have somehow slipped through a portal to late nineties Berlin and they probably won't let us in because we just don't quite get how to *feel* it with the requisite degree of earnestness. I'm about to flash Janet a look that attempts to convey all of this when I realize that she's into it already and is shaking her ass in a robotic way that I'll never pull off as she happily hands over her twenty bucks for a ticket and buck fifty for the coat check and then I realize this isn't late nineties Berlin at all, this is present tense Montreal. This is where I live. I look down at my short denim skirt with fuchsia lacy trim and my little boots and my t-shirt that's made out of a bunch of old, hilarious t-shirts cut up and sewn back together so as to accentuate my cute-though-not-astounding curves and I feel distinctly out of province but there's no leaving now, I'm here to officially pick up and I look the ticket lady in the eye and order *un billet s'il vous plait* and she doesn't give me the finger and show me the door. I take this as a good sign.

Once our jackets have been checked, I follow Janet into the place. It is huge, the size of two big highschool gyms separated into two spaces by big white pillars. One space is dotted with low, art gallery style couches as well as a few candle-lit tables with molded plastic chairs. People lounge on all of these, everyone looks languid, people smoke cigarettes, lean sexily toward each other, seemingly all are in love but on way too high a plane to acknowledge something that sentimental. I want so desperately to be part of them and am secretly pleased when Janet doesn't quite seem to belong either.

"Man, I wish we had some E," she says to me then and I blush from scalp to boots. Of course! Drugs! I am such a nerd.

The second and bigger chunk of the room is festooned with massive disco balls and is home to both the bar and the dancefloor. In the middle of the whole, sprawling space, between two of the austere white pillars is the focal point of the entire event: a tall platform overrun with electrical cords, speakers and tables behind which writhe two of the nerdiest looking, nearly dad-aged men I have ever seen. The blamming blips and bleeps and crrrrreeerrrrrrshhhhhh noises that pulse through the hall so loud I can feel them pounding in my throat are coming from these bouncing men and their machines and I'm starting to like the way the room swirls and gleams with beautiful robot future and a sexy lack of irony.

"Come on!" I say in a sudden burst of enthusiasm and a blatant desire to mate. "Let's get a drink." Janet follows, and we both crane our necks as we bop across the room, moving our hips in that almost imperceptible way we know how that says I'm not just walking down the street, I am out and I would prefer if you noticed.

We get to the bar and I have to employ my hip bones yet again to drill through the weedy mass of people all lusty for the drink, all waving their ready bills at the bitchy, sweaty bartender. "So do you want a beer or what do you—" I turn and say loudly to no one. Janet's gone. I feel stupid and again wish I wasn't wearing this shirt but the part that's worse is that no one has noticed, I might as well be wearing nothing at all, I'd make just as much of an impact.

I see Janet on the dancefloor. Oh. Talking. To a boy. Oh! Oh good. That's good! My eyes can't help themselves, they scan the crowd for his friends, he must have friends, no one comes to something like this alone do they? Do they? Ah. No, there they are a whole knot of them the boy is introducing them to Janet and she's smiling and she's giddy and they. Are all girls. And now she's caught my eye and she's waving me over and it hits me that in order to observe all of these goings on on the dance floor I have practically assumed a crouch so as to get a clear view through the mass of legs and arms and asses that are all around me and I'm squinting like a middle-aged woman who refuses to get bifocals because she's clinging to her youth. I'm still wearing these dorky clothes and now I have to straighten myself up and go over there, still without a drink and meet these people wearing black who are cool like I will never be? No no. I give Janet the "one minute" finger and disappear back into the warm throng of lushes. I push my way to the front, with force now, elbows not hips and order my beers in French to try to save face.

Take a deep breath, walk over, excuse me excuse me excuse me, expertly weaving and then, sunnily, "Hi! I thought I'd lost you!" Very nice.

"Kate! Sorry, I just ran into Richard. Richard this is Kate, my friend from work, Kate this is Richard, he's an old friend of mine from highschool." Janet looks pleased as proverbial punch. I can't help but be happy about her boysmile.

"Cool, hi," I say. "Um. Here's your beer."

She takes it and we stand in a circle and people just move and talk and yelp and dance all around and I had forgotten, I had so forgotten what it was like. Before Brian. I drink way too fast, the cool keeping me calm and the dancers are into it, some clearly amphetamined, some blurry and drunk, all of them pulsing their limbs around with an economy I don't think I can muster, my dance style being generally antithetical to computers.

Though Janet keeps trying to bring me into the conversation, they drift off on their own from time to time and I don't mind because it's fizzing. It's cracking. There are sparks. And I'm insanely jealous, yes, and it was supposed to me, yes, and where the fuck is karma when Janet just screwed me over on the fucking weekend and now she's getting some play but oh. This is it. Isn't it?

"I'm going to get another drink kay dudes?" I say, "You guys want anything?"

They don't. I do a shot of vodka, buy another beer and it's half gone before I get back onto the dancefloor but you know those nights when you drink and drink and you just don't get drunk, just kind of heavy? There's someone talking about that kind of night every morning at the Cup, somebody complaining that they just couldn't get shitfaced the night before, well this time it's me. That's okay, I don't need it, but I might need it to dance and I came here to dance but I.

I look up at the platform where they're switching dorky men and this set is accompanied by a woman with huge hair crooning into a microphone. It's the perfect altar for such a committed congregation, the Apple symbols on the matching laptops the musicmakers manipulate like two perfect jewels as archetypal and symbolic as the cross. Or maybe like two parasitic, corporate sores on the undulating, opiated skin of the masses. I may not be drunk but I'm melodramatic and bloated.

I make my way back and Janet and Richard are dancing with some pretty French girls. I come over and smile at them and try really hard to look nonchalant about trying to get the beat, trying to trick my body into moving more mechanically than it wants to. Janet comes over to me and I realize this is the first time we've danced together. I hope I'm not letting her down, this can be a big step for a girl-girl relationship. I think bigger than kissing on the lips.

"Hey, I'm really sorry for ignoring you," Janet whispers into my ear that's bouncing up and down.

"No no! Don't worry," I say. "He's really cute."

"I know!" she squeals, "And he broke up with the girl-friend he had forever."

"Wicked! Hey, are you drunk?" I ask suddenly.

"No. But we smoked a joint while you were gone. I tried to find you, but I couldn't see you anywhere."

"Yeah. I'm not really all here."

"Are you okay?"

"Yeah, yeah, totally. It's. It's just not my night I guess."

A shadow goes over Janet's face, taking away her crazy smile for a moment. "It's not Brian is it?" she asks.

Stuff stops. The music, the dancing, the smoke machine, the disco balls, the voices, the French, the fact that this is Montreal, my quest to stitch myself securely into this new life, all of it stands still. Is it? Is it? I have a queasy belly and then a dizzy head and I picture myself going home to him, putting my arms around him and, yes, I'd like it, but is it him? Is that what this is? Is he why it's not my night?

"I don't know," I say and the bass kicks back in and I real-ize I haven't stopped dancing, nothing stopped at all. "I think I'm just tired. I might just go home."

"What? No! Are you sure? Is it Richard? I can say you were feeling sick, we can go somewhere else if you want."

"No way, are you kidding?" I look over at Richard who waves a high wave, closes his eyes, whacks his head around to the music like a happy, bemuscled android.

"I'm sorry, I'm just having a really good time."

"Totally! Oh my God, totally stay. It's nothing to do with you, don't worry. I'm just so happy he's not Lee!"

"Yeah," Janet says and I watch this thought spread in her like food colouring in water, "yeah, fuck Lee!" she says and giggles and I giggle too and we do a couple of super retarded, extra-high irony dance moves together with mega eye contact, we work it out. Because we know.

"So you're really gonna go then?" she asks.

"I think so, I'll get a cab."

Janet and I hug and I wave goodbye to Richard and I watch them dance together and I wriggle my way through the crowd and I see some boys look at me as I leave, not just making fun of my t-shirt either, I see one in particular, a blond one, I could do it, I could go up to him and ask him for the time and I could talk about the music if I wanted and I could make jokes to see if they'd take, but man. I'd like to go to bed.

In the cab I look out the window and the city comes into focus. I see Ste. Catherine street with all its sleazy strip clubs and crappy restaurants and clothing stores and when I peer up the sidestreets I see the mountain, dimly lit this time of night, but there all the time. Something special. Something that I want to make a part of me. My cab driver is silent, just drives and stops at lights, then drives again. We get going pretty fast at one point and I can feel the road thundering underneath us, shooting back behind us and unspooling out in front like some kind of a hackneyed metaphor for journey and quest. And then we stop at the lights.

When I get home, my downstairs neighbour Jimmy is smoking cigars on the front steps with a short, stout guy with crazy red hair and the girl I saw feeding the squirrel. Her cigar makes her look cartoonish, but her posture's still great and she's really well dressed.

"Hey," I say as I start up the stairs. It's only one-thirty in the morning, but I'm exhausted. "I really like your skirt," I say to the girl.

"Thanks," she says back.

"Hey listen," says Jimmy, who's shirtless in spite of the fact that it's only fifteen degrees. "You know that guy who's always fucking yelling?"

I stop my climb. I step down a step.

"John."

"You know him?"

"A little," I say.

"Well, we called the landlord today, we're gonna try and get him out. The thing is, we need more complaints right, because if it's only two of us, it's not enough."

"Why do you want him out?" I say as evenly as I can. I think of John in his green briefs, out on the fire escape. Out? I'm glad I'm not drunk or I might not be able to calmly evaluate the acid glow in my belly as the just-kindled fire of war.

"Um, because he's totally nuts and he freaks the hell out of me?" Suddenly the girl, in her very expensive, pretty skirt, has a surprisingly loud voice that slices through the night like ice. She sucks on her cigar for a severed second, then continues. "I mean, we don't have to deal with that shit. Like, that guy needs some serious help."

"Yeah," I say. "And I'm sure he'll get just the help he

159

needs when he's out on the streets."

I know my voice is bitchy, I don't really care. Fight, flight or fuck. "Fight" has finally hit me for the very first time. Who the fuck do these piece of shit kids think they are, moving into this building with their parents' money and their fat student loans and their futons and Ikea chairs. Oh I know I'm describing myself, too, I see it, I get the joke, I just referenced my acting class for Christ's sake, but fuck. It sucks. *I* suck, too, whatever, fine, but right now they suck more and I stare this girl down because I want to. I really want to. I am ready for whatever she gives me.

"What are you, a socialist?"

I snort, loud, like a bull. I mean I *snort*. "I'm just not a bitch."

And she gets up. Holy shit! But I'm not that scared. Fight. Because it matters. She stands on the step above mine and I look right up into her pretty blue eyes and she stares down into mine and I hear Jimmy say "holy shit" to the other guy and she takes a puff of her rank cigar and she blows the smoke into my face but I don't even blink. Fight. I'm not tired any more, my heart is pounding and I look at her face and it looks like meat. It seems like forever that we're locked like that and the smoke swirls between us and there is hate and utter tension.

Then she cuts the string. "Come on, let's go to the Cock and Bull," she says to Jimmy and their henchman. She shoulders past me and they walk away, to go get drunk and call me ugly and stupid.

I'm shaking and I feel cold and small as the adrenaline ebbs but I feel a surge of pride that lightens my steps the three flights up to my apartment because I was ready. As ready for anything as I could ever be.

Wrapped up in bed I drink some mint tea, trying to let the last dregs of fight drain out of me so that I can go to sleep. I don't bother to take off my makeup and my going out clothes lie in a heap on the floor. I think of Janet, falling in love at the SAT. Love packing another sucker into its meatgrinder gears and turning the crank. It'll be sad to see a red and pulpy Janet come out on the other side. But maybe this one will be better. I suppose there's always hope. Maybe Janet is smarter than me and won't chase it forever. But I just can't help myself.

I used to go find Brian at school when we had first started dating. Every day I would tell myself to just leave him alone, just let him do his work, but I would want to see him so badly. I let him become as necessary to me as food, I just wouldn't feel good if I didn't see him at least once a day, didn't have a story from him or a joke to go to bed with, to smile at dumbly till dreams of him scooped me up. I was like a deranged butterfly catcher chasing him, swiping and grabbing at him, making little, squirming pieces of him mine, bringing them home, ramming pins through them just to keep them down, to make them stop, to make him stay. Forever. That was all I wanted. And every day, every time I did finally catch him at the library, at the English reading room, at the Tim Hortons, I was always in a state of panic, harried that I may have missed him, that I might not see him today, and when I finally did see him, bent over a book, so fully there, so in the work, playing with a piece of dirty hair,

I would feel it wash over me again: love. It would be all I could do not to sigh out those words, the big ones, "I love you!" But I knew better than that when he turned around to see me, smiled hi, touched my wrist. Those words would come out of me and they would not be returned and then they'd just be everywhere, all over the walls, the floors, in my hair, on Brian's shirt like I'd exploded a jar of jam. So I'd keep them in and beam at him and we'd have a walk through the library and finally I'd be as fully somewhere as Brian was when he did his work.

I was crazy. I don't deny it. I *felt* crazy. Because I knew that it wasn't the same for him. I knew that and that's what drove me faster and harder. I *knew* so how could I be so stupid? It's like when you stay in bed until three o'clock and there's that fight between intense guilt that your day is being frittered away in the big fatty pan of your bed and the absolute bliss you are feeling under your warm, warm blankets, the feeling of your cool cotton sheets against your warm, happy feet, moving your legs around under all that joy a big half of you wonders what about this could possibly be wrong? That's what it was like.

God, I could go on forever. I might. I probably will. But I'm really, really tired. I want to go to sleep. Don't kid yourself, I highly doubt I'm done. The climax here is revealing itself to be of the multiple variety, in case you didn't already know, in case *Cosmo* didn't tell you. Again and again and again and again and again and again and again... I really could go on forever.

Acknowledgments

I would like to thank the following people: Andy Brown for being a fantastic, caring, cutting-edge publisher, and a great designer, for believing in my stuff and for buying me lunch; Trevor Ferguson for listening, great criticism and teaching me to use commas; Maggie for so much inspiration, support and friendship and for being the best PR person a lady could ask for; Allison for believing in me and telling me stories on the phone; Dimitri for so many kind words of wisdom, both as a great writer and as my bud; Eva for nerding things out with me till they were better; Nick for supporting this book's shortness; Andrew for many years of writing help and fabulous hair; my Montreal neighbours for living there and being lovely; Aline for reading this book in Singapore; Concordia's prose workshop 2002 for loving doughnuts; Jesse and Maggie for super muffin art; Brigitte and Gary for being the best; and Mr. Ford for telling me to pick the right details.

Julia Tausch sometimes lives in Montreal, sometimes in Toronto. She recently completed her MA in English Literature and Creative Writing at Concordia University. Previously she has been published in *The Cyclops Review*, *Matrix*, and *Career Suicide: Contemporary Literary Humour*. She won the J.C.W. Saxon Award for playwriting in 2001. This is her first novel.